DARK WATERS

Dark Waters
is published by Stone Arch Books,
a Capstone imprint
1710 Roe Crest Drive
North Mankato, Minnesota 56003
www.mycapstone.com

Library of Congress Cataloging-in-Publication Data
Names: Gilbert, Julie, 1976- author. | Fagan, Kirbi, illustrator.
Title: Fire and Ice : a mermaid's journey / by Julie Gilbert ; illustrated by Kirbi Fagan.
Description: North Mankato, Minnesota : Stone Arch Books, an imprint of Capstone Press, [2017]
  | Series: Dark waters |
Summary: Sent to Maine to spend the summer with her grandfather, India Finch has just
  learned that she is part-mermaid, and met her kin among the Ice Tribe, so when she finds
  out that someone is harming sea creatures she wants to help – but discovering the truth can
  be dangerous, especially when the threat comes from the Mer themselves.
Identifiers: LCCN 2016032900| ISBN 9781496541680 (library binding) | ISBN 9781496541727 (pbk.)
  | ISBN 9781496541765 (ebook pdf)
Subjects: LCSH: Mermaids–Juvenile fiction. | African Americans–Juvenile fiction. |
  Grandfathers–Juvenile fiction. | Friendship–Juvenile fiction. | Conspiracies–Juvenile fiction. |
  Secrecy–Juvenile fiction. | Maine–Juvenile fiction. | CYAC: Mermaids–Fiction. | African
  Americans–Fiction. | Grandfathers–Fiction. | Friendship–Fiction. | Conspiracies–Fiction. |
  Secrets–Fiction. | Maine–Fiction.
Classification: LCC PZ7.1.G549 Fi 2017 | DDC 813.6 [Fic] –dc23
LC record available at https://lccn.loc.gov/2016032900

Designer: Hilary Wacholz

Printed in the United States of America.
010019S17

FIRE AND ICE

A MERMAID'S JOURNEY

by JULIE GILBERT

illustrated by KIRBI FAGAN

STONE ARCH BOOKS
a capstone imprint

My name is India Finch. People say it's a funny name. India is a country, and a finch is a kind of bird. A country and a bird. It's an odd name for someone who is a mermaid. Well, part mermaid.

Confused? Me too. I didn't know I was part-mermaid until this summer. I'm spending the summer with my grandpa on the coast of Maine. It's beautiful here. Lots of pine trees and wild, rocky beaches. And the ocean is amazing. The sea stretches forever and ever. The waves crash against the rocks.

The ocean makes me feel huge and small at the same time. It feels like home.

I was shocked when Grandpa told me he was part mer. I thought he was joking. Turns out he wasn't. Grandpa's mother was a mermaid. He's part-mer, and so am I.

On the outside, I look like an ordinary girl. I have medium brown skin, dark brown eyes, and crinkly dark hair. I get my stubborn chin from my mom and my crooked ears from my dad. I'm tall for my age, and my arms and legs are strong.

I look like an ordinary girl in the water too. When I'm in the ocean, I don't grow a tail or gills. But salt water makes my mer abilities wake up. I can breathe water instead of air. I can also swim for miles and miles without getting tired. And I can use my hands to heal injuries and illnesses. I have extra powers because I'm female. All mermaids have powers, but none of the mermen do.

My mermaid friends have amazing powers too.

Nari can talk to sea creatures using her mind. She can communicate with fish and lobsters and seals.

She says the sea creatures make better friends than most of the mer.

Dana can make water thick. When she does, I feel like I'm swimming in clear jelly. She likes to tease us sometimes. We'll be swimming along, and suddenly the water is too thick to move.

Lulu can move currents and make waves. She's really strong, just like her personality. I shouldn't have favorites, but I like Lulu the best. She's a fighter, like me. Or at least how I want to be.

The mer used to live all over the oceans. That's why so many cultures have stories about mermaids, even though people don't believe in mermaids. It's funny that humans don't know the mer are real. Humans are to blame for so many mer problems, after all.

Mer homes have always been protected by domes. The domes are like giant snow globes that make whatever is inside them invisible. The dome forms naturally when the mer live in harmony with their surroundings. Once people started drilling for oil, laying cables, and polluting oceans, mer homes were destroyed. The domes protecting the mer collapsed.

The mer started to die out. The remaining mer banded together and formed two tribes. Even though the tribes don't always get along, the mer are safer together than apart.

Almost three hundred mer live in these two tribes in the canyons off the coast of Maine. My mermaid friends are part of the Ice Canyon tribe. The other tribe is the Fire Canyon tribe. Neither tribe likes humans.

The Ice Canyon tribe wants to leave the humans alone. Live and let live, they say. The Fire Canyon mer are different. They want to attack humans and punish them.

Members from the different tribes aren't supposed to hang out with each other. This means I can't spend as much time with Evan as I'd like to. He's one of the Fire Canyon mer. He's also really smart — and cute. He seems to like me too.

I don't know how long I'll be able to hang out with Evan or any of my friends. Grandpa told me that when he was a young man, he had to choose between living on land or in the sea.

He had fallen in love with my grandmother. She was human. Because of her, Grandpa chose land. But he promised that his children and grandchildren would always help the mer.

Unfortunately my dad wanted nothing to do with the mer. He used to swim with them when he was my age, but then something happened. Dad made a bad decision, and a mermaid died. I don't know the whole story and neither does Grandpa.

When he was old enough, Dad moved to the middle of the country. Grandpa said Dad wanted to keep me away from the ocean while I was growing up. As a kid, I never knew I was part-mer. But I think Dad wanted me to know. Right before I got on the plane, Dad took me by the shoulders.

"Trust Grandpa," he said. "Whatever he says. No matter how crazy it sounds."

Then he hugged me tight and walked away.

I didn't know what Dad meant until I came to Maine and discovered my mer abilities. I still don't know if my mom knows. Even if Dad told her, I'm not sure she'd believe him.

The first time I talked with Dad on the phone, I asked him about the mer. I told him how shocked I was to learn the news. And that I wanted to know everything.

"We'll talk about it when you get home," was all he said.

I like being with the mer. They call me when they need my help by sending a seaweed wreath. Then I jump into the ocean to be with my friends.

Because I'm half-human, the dome makes it impossible for me to find the canyons on my own. The canyons are invisible to me until I'm inside the dome.

My human eyes can't see the dome, either, although it's supposed to be beautiful. My friends have to take me to and from the canyons where the mer live.

We have lots of wild adventures. Sometimes, though, I wonder if the mer only like me because of my powers. After all, I'm the only one who has healing powers. Would they even want me around if I couldn't help them?

I also wonder what my future holds. Will I have to make the same choice Grandpa did? Will I have to choose between my human side and my mermaid side? I'm not sure. I don't know which side I'd pick.

Maybe one day I'll know for sure.

CHAPTER 1

The ocean is green today. Yesterday it was gray. This morning it was pink and gold in the sunrise. I used to think the ocean was only blue.

You can't blame me. I grew up in Ohio. It's about as far away from the ocean as you can get. But I'm learning that the ocean is always changing.

Every day of this weird, strange summer, I learn something new. I now know how to tie a knot in the shape of a heart. I can dock a boat. I can catch a fish. I can clean that fish and cook it over a campfire.

I wonder if my friends back home will recognize me in the fall. They're all at swim camp this summer. I should be there too. And I should be with my mom and dad. At the thought of my parents, my heart rips in two. I text my parents every day, at least when I'm in town and can get a signal. I miss them so much.

I know they miss me too, even though they sent me here. They have been fighting a lot. They never told me directly, but I know they are thinking about separating. That's the real reason I'm in Maine with Grandpa, learning how to become a mermaid. I hope they work through their problems this summer. I wonder what kind of home I'll have at the end of August.

I glance at the ocean beneath my feet. The waves crash against the base of the rocks. A seaweed wreath is at my feet. The wreath is the signal my mermaid friends send when they need me. It means they are in trouble. I need to get to them as fast as possible. I get into a diving crouch and swing my arms. I do the same thing when I'm starting a swim race.

My jump is interrupted by a loud voice.

"Hey!" A man is shouting at me. He's on the beach behind me. His hand is cupped around his mouth. The wind is taking his words away. He starts to climb over the rocks toward me. "Hey, you!"

"What do you want?" I demand. I don't know this man. I don't know why he's shouting at me. And I don't like the way he is climbing toward me.

The man is out of breath when he reaches me. Up close, I see that he's my dad's age. He even looks a little like my dad, except my dad's skin is dark brown. This man's skin is pale. His cheeks are sunburned.

"You can't be out here," he says.

"Why not?" I demand.

"It's not safe," the man says. He places his hands on his knees. He's still trying to catch his breath.

A nametag hangs from his shirt. It says Beach Patrol and that his name is Officer Kevin. "It is for me," I say.

This is true. If I jumped into the water right now, I would be fine. I can breathe underwater and swim for miles.

I can't let him see me do this, though. Humans can't know mermaids are real.

"No," he's saying. "The tides are dangerous here. Kids have drowned. Not in a long time, but it's still dangerous."

"I wasn't going to dive into the water," I lie.

"You're not even supposed to be out here," Officer Kevin says. "These rocks are off limits."

"How would I know that?" I say.

He frowns at me. "Didn't you see the signs?" He points to where the rocks meet the sand.

I look where he's pointing and see the back of a sign. I've passed it many times. But I've never really noticed it.

"Those signs say keep off the rocks," Officer Kevin is explaining. "Now you need to leave." He waves at me. I don't move.

"What's going on here?" a voice says.

I sigh. I know that voice.

Officer Kevin jumps. "You scared me," he says.

My grandpa appears behind him. He must have climbed up the north side of the rocks. No wonder we didn't see him sooner.

"Officer Kevin," Grandpa says, nodding his head. Grandpa may live by himself in a cabin, but he believes in good manners.

"Mr. Finch. Good to see you. What are you doing out here?" Officer Kevin glances between me and Grandpa. He's noticing how my skin is only a few shades lighter than Grandpa's dark brown skin. He sees how my hair is kinky and thick, like Grandpa's. My hair is black, though. Grandpa's is white.

"Is this your granddaughter?" Officer Kevin asks. He looks surprised.

"Yes. This is India," Grandpa explains. "She's staying with me for the summer. Visiting from Ohio."

"Oh," Officer Kevin says. He turns back to me. "I didn't know you had grandkids, Adam."

"Just the one," Grandpa says. "You didn't grow up here. You wouldn't have known my son Jamal — India's father."

"I see," Officer Kevin nods. "Well, India, just be sure to stay off these rocks. Especially since you're new to the ocean."

"I'll make sure she's careful," Grandpa says.

Officer Kevin waves at us and climbs back to the beach. Grandpa waits until Officer Kevin is around the bend before he says anything.

"You were careless," Grandpa scolds.

"I didn't know the rocks were off limits," I say.

"I'm not worried about the rocks. I know you are safe out here. What if Kevin had seen you jump?" Grandpa asks.

"He didn't see me," I protest.

"But what if he had?" Grandpa demands. "He would have looked for you. He would have thought you had drowned. How would you have explained it if Officer Kevin found you safe and sound? These rocks are dangerous for humans."

I frown. Shame creeps over me. "I wasn't trying to be careless," I say.

Grandpa takes my arm and gives it a shake.

"No one can know about the mermaids, India," he says. "No one. If the humans knew about mermaids, it would ruin everything."

"Don't you think I know that? You've been telling me that ever since I started visiting Ice Canyon," I say.

"You need to understand the danger," Grandpa says. "Do you know how the dome is maintained?"

"Something about the animals," I mumble. I'm hazy on the details.

"The mer live in perfect harmony with their surroundings. That includes the sea creatures who live in the canyons. This balance creates the dome. It's an old, powerful magic. If anything messes with that harmony, the balance will be destroyed. The dome will disappear. The mer will be exposed."

"What makes you so sure humans will bother the mer even if that happens?" I ask. "Maybe humans wouldn't care. Maybe they would leave the mer alone."

Grandpa snorts. "Would leave them alone? Pretend you're not part-mer. Someone discovers mermaids are real. Would you just ignore the news?"

I think about it. "I guess not," I say. "It would be like learning that unicorns exist. I'd want to see one."

"That's why you have to be careful," Grandpa repeats. "You understand?"

"I told you, I know!" I jerk my arm free from his grasp. We look at each other for a long moment. I'm angry.

Grandpa looks sad. Then his face softens. "I know you are trying to be safe, India," he says. "Can you blame me for worrying?"

I don't know what to say. My mom says the same thing to me sometimes.

"Just be careful," Grandpa says. "Don't let Officer Kevin or anyone else see you out here."

"I won't," I grumble.

Just then Grandpa notices the seaweed wreath at my feet. "They called you," he says.

"Yes. That's why I came out here," I say.

Grandpa glances over his shoulder. The beach is empty, but soon it will be busy, even though it is a Tuesday.

"You might be gone for a while," Grandpa says. When I visit the mer, I might be gone for days or even a week or two. I'm not quite used to having so much freedom. In Ohio, I have to be home by dark.

"Depends on what they need me to do," I say. "But they'll send reports." Whenever I'm gone for more than a few days, Ani sends someone to tell Grandpa. They send a wreath and everything. Grandpa knows to go to the cliffs for an update.

"I will watch for a wreath, then," Grandpa says.

I stand awkwardly in front of him. "Well, then. Guess I should be going."

"India, you will always have a home with me when you return," Grandpa says in a rush. "Now go." He gives me a nudge. "Go help your friends."

I don't hug Grandpa. He is not much of a hugger. Instead I smile and say thank you. Then I go to the edge of the cliffs and jump in.

CHAPTER 2

Every time I go into the water, I remember the first time I met my friends.

Grandpa told me about the mermaids on one of my first days here. I didn't believe him. How could his mother be a mermaid? Wouldn't I have noticed that I was part-mer before this?

Eventually Grandpa told me to go to sleep. I dreamed of mermaids that night, but I still didn't believe him.

The next morning we went down to the water. The sun was warm, but the wind was cool. The breeze tasted like salt.

"Out there," Grandpa said. He pointed at the rocks jutting into the ocean. The same ones that Officer Kevin would later tell me were off limits.

"Okay," I said. I climbed over the rocks behind him.

"Now jump," Grandpa said. We stood on the edge of the rocks.

I looked back at the beach. It was farther away than I'd thought. Waves crashed at my feet.

"You want me to jump into the ocean," I said.

"Yes," Grandpa confirmed.

"I didn't wear my swimsuit." I pointed at my shorts and T-shirt.

"Doesn't matter. Jump anyway," he repeated.

Enough was enough. "Grandpa, this is weird," I said. "I'm not jumping into the ocean. I don't care what you say about your mom. She wasn't a mermaid. Neither am —"

I didn't get a chance to finish my sentence. Grandpa took me by the shoulders and tossed me into the water.

"Sorry, India!" I heard him call. Then I sank beneath the waves.

I have always been a good swimmer. I had never swum in the ocean, though. This was different. This was not the same as high school pools or even Lake Erie. In the ocean, the currents are strong.

I got pulled and pushed in opposite directions. I got water in my mouth. I was about to drown in the ocean.

Wake up, India! I told myself. I started kicking my legs. I saw light above my head. I swam in that direction, figuring the light was the surface.

After a few moments, I stopped swimming. I should have been at the surface. Instead I was near the bottom of a rocky cliff.

I looked around. A lobster tiptoed past me. I blinked and rubbed my eyes. For a second it looked like the lobster waved before it walked away.

This was my first time in the ocean. *Shouldn't my eyes burn from the salt?* I thought. Instead everything looked clear, even though I wasn't wearing goggles.

A school of silver fish swam past. I got the strange urge to follow them. I pushed off from the rock cliff and swam. Only then did I realize I was breathing underwater. Instead of air, I was taking in water through my nose and mouth. But I wasn't drowning.

I felt shocked and started to panic. My arms and legs jerked. The fish were gone. I could not see the rock cliff. I was lost in the ocean.

Then a pair of strong hands closed around my shoulders and lifted me up. "First time?" a musical voice asked.

I turned around. I found myself looking into the face of a girl my own age. Her skin was a few shades darker than mine. Her hair was crinkly and black. It floated in the water above her head.

"Who are you?" I asked. I realized I was speaking as clearly as if we were talking on land.

"My name is Lulu," she said. "What's yours?"

"India Finch," I said.

"Nice to meet you, India Finch," Lulu said with a smile.

She turned slightly, and that's when I realized she had a tail. From the waist up she looked like a normal girl. She wore a short-sleeved shirt that came down to her hips. But instead of legs, she had a giant fish tail. Her tail was beautiful, dark green.

I gasped. "You're a mermaid!"

"Of course," Lulu said. She smiled. "What did you think I was?"

"I've never met a mermaid before," I said.

"Well, here are some more," she said.

I turned and saw two more mermaids swimming toward us. They were both smiling.

"Hi, I'm Dana," the one with white skin and red hair said. "This is Nari."

"Hello," Nari said. She had long black hair and looked like my friend Amy, who'd been born in Korea. She also had a blue striped tail and sparkly fins.

"Hey," I said. My voice was weak.

"This is her first time meeting mermaids," Lulu said with a smile.

"We've seen you before," Dana said. Her bright pink tail almost glowed underwater. "Your grandpa sent us a wreath of flowers a few weeks ago. We guessed a new Finch had arrived to help us. I saw you on the beach. I wanted to wave, but there were other people around. We're not supposed to let humans see us."

"Okay," I said. I felt like I was dreaming. This was too weird.

"So you're Adam Finch's granddaughter?" Lulu asked.

"You know Grandpa?" I asked.

"We've never met him," Nari said. She had a low, sweet voice. "But we know who he is. His mother was a mermaid."

"No kidding," I said.

"You didn't know we existed," Dana said. A teasing grin split her face.

"Not really. My dad . . ." My voice trailed off.

"My mom told me he used to visit," Lulu said. "When he was younger. I don't think it ended well."

"What happened?" I asked. I was eager to hear any news about my dad. I still couldn't believe he had never said anything about the mer when I was growing up.

"We're part of the Ice Canyon tribe of mermaids," Lulu explained. "Another tribe lives nearby. The Fire Canyon tribe. The tribes used to argue a lot more when everyone first moved here. That was when your dad visited. He got caught in the middle of a fight."

"Did he get hurt?" I asked.

"No, but a mermaid did," Lulu replied. "She died."

"What?" I cried, horrified.

"I don't know the whole story," Lulu said.

Nari poked Lulu's arm. "We need to get back. Your mom is waiting for us."

"Wait, I have so many questions," I said.

"We know," Dana said, squeezing my hand. "You'll see us again. We'll send you a signal. A wreath of seaweed. Look for it. Then meet us here."

"Can you help me find the surface?" I asked.

Dana grinned. "Sure. You'll get used to finding your way after a few times, but it's confusing at first."

The mermaids led me to the surface. Just below the water, they all gave me hugs before swimming away. Even though I could see clearly in the ocean, it wasn't long before they disappeared from sight.

When I got back from that first visit, I asked Grandpa why he had sent a wreath to the mer.

"The wreath told them the Finch family hasn't forgotten our promise," he explained. "I let them know that you were here. The Finch family is ready to help them when they are in trouble."

I patted my hair dry. "I still don't understand why we need to help the mer."

"They are family, India," he said. "That's what family does. And since you are female, you will have powers that can help them even more than I can."

"Why don't the mermen have powers?" I asked.

Grandpa shrugged. "It is the way of the mer. The females have always had additional powers."

"What are mine?" I asked.

"You'll figure it out," was all he said. "I'm sure you'll figure it out."

He wasn't going to tell me anything more. I tried a different approach. "What happened when Dad went into the ocean?" I asked.

Grandpa frowned. "I never got the whole story from him. He came home with a broken arm."

"They said he got caught in the middle of a fight," I said. "Someone said a mermaid died."

Grandpa sighed. "I wondered if something like that had happened. All I know is he never went back."

"Didn't they want him to go back? You said you promised them that the Finch family would always help," I said.

"After your dad's visit, the mer never asked for help again. I didn't even send the wreath until this summer to let them know you were here," Grandpa said.

And since my first visit, I've walked the beach every day looking for seaweed wreaths. Whenever I find them, I jump in and help the mermaids. Because we are family.

CHAPTER 3

I shake my head to clear it of memories. I'm in the ocean, and even though I'm part-mermaid, I still have to pay attention to tides and currents. Officer Kevin is right. The tides near the rock cliff are dangerous. I knew this already, but it was a good reminder.

In a few moments, my eyes and lungs adjust to being underwater. I look around. The mermaids are waiting for me.

"How's it going?" Lulu asks, grinning at me. Nari and Dana both hug me.

"I've missed you," I say, hugging them back. "What's going on?"

Lulu makes a face. "We'll get to that. First we'll take you to Ice Canyon."

We fly through the water. A pod of dolphins swims with us. I wonder if Nari is talking with them. With her special power she can communicate with sea creatures. She sends them images through her mind. They reply the same way.

The journey is exciting. I love being in the deep waters. I'm full-on laughing by the time we get close to Ice Canyon. We pass schools of tuna and cod, not to mention lobsters and sea scallops. Sometimes we swim with seals. One time I saw a humpback whale, which was huge. I kept a safe distance.

The only creatures we really have to watch out for are sharks and giant squid. They are the only animals that prey on mermaids. If a shark or squid ever attacked us, Nari couldn't even send it away. She can't communicate with the creatures that hunt us.

As we approach, I see the guards. Ice Canyon has guards at all the entrances. They watch the dome and keep an eye on activity outside the dome, like when humans get close.

This is one reason why I can't go to Ice Canyon on my own. Even if I could find the canyons by myself, some of the guards wouldn't let me in. A few of the guards like me enough. They might let me pass. But it's safer for me to go with my mermaid friends.

"India's with us so you're going to let her in," Lulu tells the guards.

The guard scowls at me when I swim past. In his eyes, the human part of me outweighs the mer part.

"It's not personal," Nari says, linking her arm through mine.

"I know," I say. We've discussed this many times. A lot of the mer don't like me because I'm part-human. "It feels personal, though."

"They'll come around," Dana says. "Your healing powers are so important to us. A lot of mer are starting to see that."

"I wish they'd see it sooner," I say. "Are we inside the dome yet?"

"We just passed through it," Nari says. "It's mainly gold today with streaks of lavender."

I wish again that I could see the dome. From the way my friends describe how the colors swirl and dance, it sounds like an underwater version of the Northern Lights.

I forget the guard as we swim into Ice Canyon. The place never fails to take my breath away. The canyons are a series of cliffs bigger than the Grand Canyon. The rocks are covered in beautiful coral in pinks and purples and browns. Piles of flat rocks lie near the base of the canyons.

The cliffs rise above us. Mer homes are marked by openings in the cliffs. Two mermaids swim out of one of the caves and look down at us. When they see me, they both frown and swim away.

"Sorry," Lulu says. For some reason, her apology makes me laugh. Soon we are all laughing.

"At least you have us, right?" Dana says. We hold hands and swim through the canyon. Other mer peek at us. Only one mermaid smiles at me. She has greenish skin and long dark hair. Her tail is the color of olives.

"Who's that?" I ask. "I've never seen her before."

"Her name is Sirene," Lulu says.

"Sirene doesn't live in Ice Canyon," Dana explains.

"She's a Fire Canyon mermaid?" I ask.

"No," Nari says. Her long black hair streams behind her. "She doesn't have a tribe."

"I didn't know mer lived without a tribe," I say.

"Sirene does. She shows up a few times a year for news. Then she heads right back out again," Lulu says.

"She gives up the protection of the tribes, though," Nari says. "And she doesn't have a dome to hide her."

"What is she doing all by herself?" I ask.

"No one knows," Dana says. "There are a few mer who prefer being alone to living with the tribes."

"Living in a tribe is obviously more fun," Lulu says with a wink.

She's right. Mer life is simple and easy. The ocean provides shelter and food. The mer don't need cars or buses. The only work they do is weaving blankets from seaweed, but that doesn't take much time. Guards protect them from sharks and humans.

The younger mer don't even have to go to school. They don't have a written language, so they don't need to read or write. They learn what they need to know about mer life from each other. I'm jealous of them when I think of the biology class I'll be facing next fall.

The mer aren't lazy, though. They explore the ocean. And they are storytellers and singers. Some of the stories can last for hours. The songs are beautiful too. It is so different from the life I have on land.

"I wonder if she's lonely," I say. Being in Maine gets a little lonely for me. I don't know anyone except Grandpa. I spend every day by myself when I'm not with the mer.

"Maybe," Lulu says.

Soon we reach a large cave at the base of the canyon. Two mermaids stand guard.

"We're here to see my mother," Lulu says.

"She's waiting for you," the guard with the yellow hair says. The one with the purple hair glares at me.

"It's really not you," Nari says. "It's the *idea* of humans that they don't like. Even part-mer ones."

"I know," I say.

"Humans have destroyed our homes," Dana reminds me. "The mer used to live all over the ocean. Then humans came. First we had to escape their fishing nets. Then they made the water dirty, forcing us to live together for greater protection."

"I'm sorry," I say. I know the oceans are polluted. Oil spills and chemicals and garbage have all harmed the water. I learned about it growing up. But this is the first time I've felt connected to the problems. I feel sad and ashamed.

"India! I'm so happy you're here!" Ani, Lulu's mother, swims to me and gives me a hug. At least someone other than my friends is happy to see me.

Ani looks like an older version of Lulu. Her hair is braided in thousands of braids. They float around her head. She is the leader of the Ice Canyon tribe.

"What's the problem?" I ask. The mer only send for me when there is trouble.

Ani's face falls. "Some kind of monster is hurting sea creatures. We've rescued four seals, seven lobsters, and countless squid. They have all been cut somehow."

"I've tried talking to them, but they won't tell me anything," Nari says.

"How do you know the sea creatures are being hurt by something?" I ask. "Maybe they are having accidents."

"We're pretty sure it's on purpose," Ani says. "They have all been marked with cuts in the shape of an X."

"An X?" I ask.

"We're not sure what it means. We don't know what kind of monster does this. But the sea creatures are suffering. We're suffering too," Ani says.

"The dome?" I ask.

"Yes, exactly," Ani says, looking pleased. "You've learned a lot about mer culture since your first visit. That's good."

I don't tell her that I just learned the details about how the dome is made from Grandpa earlier today.

"The more the creatures are hurt, the more the dome weakens," Ani says. "We've increased the number of guards to watch it. How did it look when you came in?"

"Gold," Nari says. "But it looked thinner than I've ever seen it."

"We've had reports of holes north of the canyons," Ani says. "We need to stop the problem before it gets worse. The other day, a fishing boat got within a half mile of the canyons. The dome usually keeps them at least a mile away."

"That's not good," I say.

"No, it's not," Ani agrees. "We need your help. Can you heal them?"

"Of course," I say.

Ani smiles. "Wonderful. The girls have been helping. Nari calms the creatures down. Then Lulu changes the currents to guide them into a large cave."

"And I've made the water thick in front of the cave so they can't escape until they're better," Dana says.

"All we need is you," Ani says.

Out of the corner of my eye, I notice Lulu fold her arms across her chest. She looks like she's frowning. Lulu and her mother don't always get along.

Actually it's more like Lulu doesn't get along with Ani. I'm not sure Ani knows there's a problem.

"Sounds like you need all of us," I say.

Ani looks surprised. "What? Oh, of course. All of the girls are helping. But we need your help more than anything."

"Okay," I say. Lulu's frown deepens. I need to get her out of here before she gets really angry. "Let's go."

Ani takes my hands. "Good luck, India."

"Thanks," I say.

"Bye, Mom," Lulu says. Her voice is flat. I don't think Ani notices.

CHAPTER 4

I spend the morning healing animals. Whatever or whoever is harming animals doesn't care how many get hurt. I heal dozens of silver cod and lobsters. I can't count the number of jellyfish with missing tentacles. The largest animal is a dolphin, who nudges me as if to say thanks.

Nari tells the animals that it will be fine and that they can trust me. Then I put my hands on their wounds and heal them.

I can't fully explain how I heal. Ani once told me that water has healing power. Water washes away pain, cleans cuts, and takes away stress.

When I put my hands on the creatures, I think of the healing power of water. Somehow I channel these powers through my hands and into the sea creatures. Then I make them better.

Most of the animals have minor injuries. They have a broken fin or damaged tentacles. They can still use their fins, but it slows them down. They are in danger of being hurt or eaten by other creatures. I fix their broken parts.

I also heal their cuts. All of the animals have cuts in the shape of an X, just like Ani described. Most of the cuts have been made at the back of their necks. If they don't have necks, I look for the X on the sides of their bodies.

"What kind of monster would do this?" I ask Nari. I have finished healing the last creature. The turtle brushes its healed flipper against my face.

"She's thanking you," Nari says.

"You're welcome," I call after the sea turtle as it swims away.

"I hate seeing them hurt," Nari says. She brushes a strand of dark hair from her face.

"You're sure they can't tell you what's hurting them?" I ask.

"Believe me, I've tried many times," Nari says. "I can't figure it out, though. They remember right before they were hurt. Then their minds go blank. The next thing they remember is being found by one of the mer."

"Were they all found at the same place?" I ask. If they were, it might help us track down the monster.

"No. They've all been found near the canyons but not in one location. Usually we find them swimming around, looking dazed," Nari explains.

"Have you been helping to rescue them?" I ask.

"Of course," Nari says with a smile. "I've even been leading some of the teams."

"Good for you!" I say. I'm glad to hear this. Nari is quiet and shy. She doesn't think of herself as a leader. She's wrong. When Nari talks, people listen. She has good ideas and thinks carefully about what to do.

Nari blushes. "I like helping the animals. I like feeling useful."

I paste a smile on my face. I know I'm useful in Ice Canyon. I'm just not sure how useful I am on land. At least not yet.

"Lulu said we should meet her and Dana later. She has something she wants to tell us," Nari says.

"Where have they been this morning?" I ask.

Nari purses her lips. "Well, Lulu has a plan. This morning she was doing some work on it."

"A plan? For what?" I ask.

"She wants to figure out who or what's behind the attacks," Nari says. "And I want to help her."

"Isn't Ani investigating too?" I ask.

"Sure," Nari says. "But Lulu wants to do things her own way. You know how she is."

I shake my head. "I want to stop the injuries just as much as anyone," I say. "But is Lulu doing this to help the animals? Or is she doing it to impress her mom?"

Nari's look is cold. "As long as we stop the suffering, does it matter?"

"I guess not," I say. "Where are we meeting them?"

"At the *Clemmons*," Nari says.

The *Clemmons* is an old steamer ship that sank in the 1860s. The ship has tons of narrow rooms and hallways to explore. It might be creepy to hang out at a shipwreck, but everyone onboard got into lifeboats. Nobody died.

Ice Canyon and Fire Canyon mer both like to hang out at the *Clemmons*. My heart jumps. Evan might be there. He's a member of the Fire Canyon tribe, so we're not supposed to hang out, but I really like him. Going to the *Clemmons* might be my one chance of seeing him on this trip.

"Sure, if that's what you want," I say. I try to keep my voice even as I follow Nari toward the ship.

When we swim past the edge of Ice Canyon. Nari waves at the guard. The guard looks relieved to see me go.

"Evan's been asking about you," Nari says as we swim into the sea between the canyons.

"He has?" I ask. My voice squeaks.

Nari laughs.

"Maybe once or twice," she says. "And a few more times than that."

I want to ask her more, but we are almost at the *Clemmons*. I love hanging out here. I would love it even if Evan weren't here.

"You made it," Dana says, swimming up to us. She gives us both a hug and keeps her arm around Nari's shoulder.

"India was amazing. She healed all the animals," Nari says.

"I'm glad I could help," I say.

"You must be tired," Dana says. She knows that healing drains me.

"You'll have time to sleep later," Lulu says, charging up to us. Her green tail flashes. She grabs my arm. "Dana and I have been talking to the other mer this morning. We gathered everybody here to share ideas."

I swim with Lulu. Nari and Dana follow us. I want to hear Lulu's plans, but I'm also looking for Evan. Lulu notices me looking.

"Don't worry, he's here," she says.

"What? Who?" I say, trying to cover.

Lulu just shakes her head and smiles.

By now we are at the *Clemmons*. Lulu leads us to the bridge deck, where most of the young mer kids hang out. I know most of them, at least by sight. They all know me. Unlike the older mer, the younger mer don't seem to mind me as much.

I say hi to everyone. Then Lulu swims to the front of the group.

"We've all been talking about the sea monster," she says. "I want you all to tell India what you just told me."

A mer with an orange tail speaks first. "We don't know much," he says. "But none of us have seen any sign of a monster. And we all know that sea monsters don't exist."

"Most people think *mermaids* don't exist," I say. "Doesn't mean they don't."

Everyone laughs a little at my joke. I see another figure swim into the corner of my vision. I know before I even look that it's Evan.

Evan is an ordinary-looking mer. His hair is short and dark. His skin is the color of caramel. His tail is such a dark green that it looks black. But I always notice him in a crowd. I always know where he is. I can always spot him.

I smile at him, just a small smile that I reserve for Evan. He returns it. I feel all warm and bubbly inside.

"Pay attention," Lulu hisses in my ear.

I realize that other mer are talking, explaining their theories about what's hurting the creatures. Some of them think it probably *is* a monster. Others wonder if it's a shark or a giant squid, although no one thinks a shark could make an X on every animal like that.

"What if it's humans?" a mermaid asks. Her name is Melody. She has long blond hair and blue eyes. She looks like one of the dolls my mom's family always gave me for Christmas. I never liked those dolls. This might be why I've never really liked Melody.

"Why would it be humans?" I challenge.

Melody shrugs her perfect shoulders. "It just seems like the kind of thing humans would do."

Lulu grabs my arm. "No one thinks it's humans," she says. She speaks low so that only I can hear it. "Melody is just trying to make you mad."

"It's working," I say. I'm angry.

"Humans aren't behind this," Lulu says loudly enough for everyone to hear.

"How do you know?" Melody challenges.

"The coast is too far away. None of the animals are coming from that direction anyway. And no one has seen any humans in the area. They aren't behind this," Lulu says.

"Whatever," Melody says, pouting. She flicks the end of her ice blue tail. She looks annoyed.

"Not sure we can help much," the mer with the orange tail says. He turns to go. "But we'll keep looking."

Lulu looks flustered. "Are you sure? We could talk more about theories."

Orange tail looks back and shrugs. "Nothing much more to talk about," he says. "Like I said, we'll keep you posted."

The meeting breaks up after that. A lot of the mer start swimming away. Out of the corner of my eye, I notice that Melody has stayed. She is talking to Evan.

"I thought they might know more," Lulu says with a sigh. "I was wrong."

"They know the same rumors we do," Dana says.

"Yep," I say. I'm not paying attention. I'm watching Melody with Evan. She lays her hand on his arm. I feel a wave of happiness when he pulls his arm away.

"Have you heard a word we've said, India?" Dana asks.

"What?" I turn to look at my friends. They are all grinning at me. I blush. "Sorry," I say.

"Sorry for what?" Evan asks, swimming up to us. Over his shoulder, I notice Melody giving me a dirty look before she leaves.

"For nothing," I sputter.

"Uh, hi, India," Evan says. I love how his hair waves in the currents.

"Hi, Evan," I say.

"Um, can I talk to you?" he asks.

I exchange a glance with my friends. "Sure," I say. My heart starts beating a little faster. "Where should we go?"

"They can hear it too," he says, gesturing at my friends. My heart falls a little bit.

"Sure. Okay," I say.

Evan runs a hand through his hair, making it stick up in the water. "I may know someone who knows something about the attacks."

Lulu pounces on this information. "Who? What?"

"Well, it's someone from Fire Canyon," Evan says. "He won't come to you. You'd have to go to him."

"We can do that," Lulu says.

"Lulu, we're not supposed to go to Fire Canyon," Nari says in a low voice.

"I don't care about the rules," Lulu says. "We have to help the animals. And we trust Evan, right?"

Lulu looks at us. None of us disagree.

"Good," she says. "We're going to Fire Canyon. Evan, lead the way."

CHAPTER 5

There are good reasons why we're not supposed to go to Fire Canyon. And it's not just because Ani would ground all of us for a month if she found out.

Fire Canyon is different than Ice Canyon. Neither tribe likes humans, but only the Fire Canyon mer want to take action. They want to stir up tidal waves and sink ships. Anything to keep the humans away from the ocean.

The Ice Canyon mer have a different idea. They want to leave the humans alone. They have no interest in starting a war.

The Ice Canyon mer don't want humans to mess up the ocean more than they already have. But they aren't willing to harm humans to stop them.

The two tribes live close to each other because there is safety in numbers. Plus they share the benefit of the dome, which stretches over both canyons. The mer only have to live in harmony with sea creatures, not with each other, to create the dome. Some of the younger mer get along, and the leaders try to work together. But the tribes don't pretend to like each other.

So it's no surprise that we get weird looks when Evan takes us past the guards. At least this time, it's not just me getting the glares.

"They really don't like us, do they?" Dana whispers.

"I feel the same whenever I go to Ice Canyon," Evan says.

"How often do you go to Ice Canyon?" I ask.

Evan glances at me over his shoulder. "Only when you're there."

I pretend not to notice Lulu making gagging noises next to me. *She's kidding,* I think.

"Where are you taking us again?" Nari asks. Her question reminds me that I should be paying more attention to our surroundings and less attention to Evan.

"To see a friend," Evan says. "You'll know more when you get there."

Fire Canyon looks the same as Ice Canyon. The same jagged cliffs. The same caves. The same beautiful coral clinging to the side of the rock.

Evan leads us around the edge of the canyon to a dark cave. "In here," he says.

We follow him into the cave and wait for our eyes to adjust to the dimness. The cave is narrow and dark. A few glowing jellyfish light the shadows. I shiver. I'm not scared, exactly, but I don't want to go any further into the cave.

"This is Bones," Evan says.

I can barely make out the shape of a merman in front of me. As my eyes adjust, I see that he is old. His hair falls in gray ropes around his face. His white skin is weathered. He is wearing an old leather vest. His tail is the color of a cucumber.

"Nice to meet you, Mr. Bones," Nari says.

"Just Bones," he says. His voice sounds like a key turning in a rusty lock.

"Evan said you have information," Lulu says. She hovers in front of Bones. He is leaning against the wall of the cave.

"I suppose I do," Bones says.

"Tell them what you told me," Evan says.

Bones looks at the four of us. His gaze rests on me. He pushes away from the wall and swims toward me.

"So this is Adam Finch's girl." He swims a slow circle around me. Fear pools in my stomach.

"My name is India," I say.

"You're one of them," he says. His lips sneer.

My muscles tense. I'm not going to let Bones make me feel bad for being part-human.

"One of them?" I say. "You must mean one of the awesome part mer who have helped the mer like you again and again."

Bones stops swimming around me. He scowls.

"You have spirit," he says. "I'll give you that."

"Bones, be nice," Evan warns.

Bones looks at Evan. "I'll be nice. Although it doesn't seem she needs your help."

Is Evan blushing? I wonder. I can't quite tell.

"Evan said you wanted to tell us something," Lulu says, taking charge.

"Did he?" Bones says. He gives Evan a look.

"You're not backing out of this," Evan says.

"I don't remember making a promise," Bones says. He waves his hand at us like he's trying to kick us out of the cave.

Evan looks mad. "I helped you home one night. You were having one of your spells. You couldn't remember who you were or where you lived."

I glance at my friends. We are all looking at each other. Our eyebrows are raised. And we all have the same expression on our faces. We are wondering if Bones is too strange to help us.

"Bones has spells?" Nari asks.

"Had some head injuries when I was younger," Bones says. "Sometimes they give me trouble. I can't always remember things."

"Head injuries?" Dana asks. I can see her mind working. She's trying to figure out if we can trust Bones or not.

"During one of the human wars," Evan explains quietly. "Submarines were bombing ships. Bones helped pull injured sailors to safety."

"Oh," we say. I am looking at Bones in a new light. Maybe he isn't so bad.

"I don't like to talk about it," Bones says.

Nari swims forward. "You were brave," she says. She lays her hand on his arm. "Be brave again. Can you tell us what you know about what's harming the animals?"

Bones looks at us. Then he sighs. "I don't know much," he says.

"What *do* you know?" Nari prompts.

"I was having a spell. So I'm not sure I remember it right. Or even if it happened at all," Bones says.

"Go on," Dana says. Her face is calm and focused. If she were human, she could be a scientist in a lab or a tennis player concentrating on the next lob.

"I was in a daze. I don't know where I was. But I thought I heard a voice say, 'X marks the spot.'"

"'X marks the spot'?" Lulu repeats. "What does that mean?"

"That's all I know," Bones says, leaning against the wall. He sounds defeated. "I'm tired. I need to nap. Go now."

We thank Bones. I can hear disappointment in our voices. Evan herds us out of the cave.

"I thought that would be more helpful," Evan says. He doesn't meet my eyes.

"We knew about the X," Lulu says. "Every injured creature has been cut in the shape of an X."

Evan looks horrified. "That's awful!"

"India healed them," Nari says. She prods me in the ribs, gently pushing me toward Evan.

"Cool," Evan says. His face is lit up. "Your powers are amazing."

"Thanks." Now I'm the one who's blushing.

"Bones was helpful though," Dana says.

"How so?" Nari asks.

"He said he heard someone say, 'X marks the spot,'" Dana replies.

"So?" Lulu asks.

"Unless it can talk, a monster isn't doing this," Dana explains. "Someone — probably one of the mer — is hurting the animals. It might also mean there's a place where someone is doing it."

I feel a chill. "We should get back to Ice Canyon," I say.

I think about what Dana said as we leave Fire Canyon. *Could one of the mer be harming the creatures? If so, why?* I want to ask my friends what they think.

Suddenly we hear shouts, and the water churns to our right. The shouting heads straight toward us. My friends and I grab each other's hands and turn to face the noise.

A group of mermaids and mermen have surrounded us. They are holding spears and wearing chains over their shirts.

"What's the meaning of this?" Lulu demands. Only her friends would notice the slight waver in her voice.

"Why are you doing this to my friends?" Evan is shouting. I notice that the mer have separated us from him.

"Your friends?" a voice asks. The voice is icy and dripping with disgust. A large and powerful merman swims up behind the guards. I roll my eyes.

"Hello, Storm," I say. Storm is the leader of the Fire Canyon tribe. He's also Evan's dad.

"Ah, India Finch," he says. He's the only one who ever uses my full name. He doesn't mean it as a compliment. "You're not supposed to be here."

"We have a right to be here," I say with confidence. "Evan invited us."

Storm scowls at Evan.

Evan's shoulders slump. "They're my friends, Dad."

I'm always surprised by how much Storm looks like his son. They have the same caramel skin. Evan's hair is short while Storm's hair floats around his shoulders, but both have the same dark color.

They also have the same sharp nose and bright eyes, but that's where the likeness ends. Storm is mean and a bully. Evan is the opposite.

"These girls aren't supposed to be here," Storm snarls. "The Ice Canyon mer are not allowed in our canyon."

"We're here on a diplomatic mission," Lulu blurts.

Storm raises an eyebrow at her. "A diplomatic mission?"

One of the mermen with Storm laughs. The sound is harsh.

I glare at the merman. He is big and hulking. If he were human, he would have made a good football player. I've seen him before. I think his name is Poe. He glares right back at me.

"Yes. Diplomatic," Lulu explains. "You know, when people on opposite sides meet to talk."

"And what do we need to talk about?" Storm demands.

"'X marks the spot,'" Lulu says.

Her words cause a reaction. Storm looks shocked. The mer guards watch him, not sure what to do. Poe shifts his hands on his harpoon.

Then Storm swims close to Lulu. He looks like he's going to yell at her. Then he changes his mind and swims away without a backward glance.

"That was weird," Lulu says as the guards swim away after Storm.

"I'm sorry about that," Evan says. He looks embarrassed. I feel bad for him.

"It's not your fault," I say.

"I'm the one who brought you here," he says. "And my dad is a jerk."

"Nobody's parents are perfect," I say.

Evan gives me a crooked smile. "Yeah, I guess."

"If you two are done cuddling, we should get back to Ice Canyon," Lulu snaps.

"We weren't cuddling," I protest. I wasn't even close enough to reach out and hold his hand.

"We need to go," she repeats.

I don't always understand Lulu. Dana says we are too much alike, so we clash sometimes. Nari says that Lulu is worried her mother will like me more than her own daughter. But that's impossible. I know how much Ani loves Lulu. I could never come between them, even if I wanted to.

I wave goodbye to Evan and follow my mermaid friends back to Ice Canyon.

CHAPTER 6

I spend the next few days healing sea creatures. More are coming in every day but fewer than when I started. Some of the Ice Canyon mer help Nari bring animals to me. A few of them even give me smiles and tell me that the dome is getting stronger.

Every time I visit, the mer are unfriendly when I first arrive. Then they warm to me when they see that I'm only trying to help them.

"They don't know what to make of you, do they?" a voice says.

I turn from the cod I'm healing. A mermaid floats near the entrance to the pen. Her skin is pale green, like new leaves in the spring.

"You're Sirene, right?" I say. I remember seeing her the day I arrived.

"Yes, I am," she says. She swims closer to me. "I've heard lots of stories about you, India."

"Really?" I ask.

"Everyone is talking about you," she says. "You've done a lot to help the Ice Canyon mer."

"I've helped at Fire Canyon too," I say. This is sort of true. I have had adventures that have helped Fire Canyon. Not that the mer there would ever admit it.

"I see," Sirene says. She flicks her long hair over a green shoulder.

"My friends say you don't live in a tribe," I say.

"They're right," Sirene replies.

"Why don't you live with other mer?" I ask.

"Now why would I want to do that, India Finch?" Sirene asks.

Is it my imagination or did she narrow her eyes at me? "What about the dome? Don't you need protection?" I ask.

"I don't need a silly bubble. I can protect myself," Sirene says. She flexes her hands and bolts of ice shoot from them. The shards embed themselves in the wall of the cave.

"That's impressive," I say. I edge away from her.

Sirene strokes the hard edge of a scallop shell. The gesture is similar to when my dad tests the edge of a kitchen knife with his thumb. My dad is just making sure the knife is sharp enough to cut onions. On Sirene, the gesture is creepy. My gut whispers that something's not right.

"Besides, with all of the hurt animals around here, there isn't much protection," Sirene points out. "The dome will disappear."

"Which is why I'm trying to heal them," I say. I'm annoyed. I want to get back to my work.

"These poor fish," Sirene says. "Who would do such a thing to them?"

"We're trying to figure it out," I say.

Sirene glances at me. "What do you think is happening to them?"

Her eyes linger on me a bit too long. My gut tells me not to share anything with Sirene.

"Nobody really knows anything," I say.

"But you must have ideas," she says.

"Nope," I say.

"I have another reason why I don't live with the tribes," Sirene says after a long pause.

"What's that?" I ask. I start working again as she talks, healing the cuts on a monkfish.

She looks at me for a long moment and then points to her arm. "Because of my skin color. There aren't many green mermaids around. At least not anymore."

The fish squirms in my hands. I make sure it is fully healed before letting it go.

"I've always felt different," Sirene continues. "The others made me feel different too. They would say my green skin meant that I wasn't really a mermaid."

"Huh," I say. If she wants me to talk about my own skin color and how it sometimes makes me feel different, it won't work.

"You must know what that feels like," she says.

"Not really," I say. I turn my attention to a nearby black sea bass.

Sirene swims closer. "But you are different," she says. "You aren't really a mermaid. And you're not really human, either."

I kick my feet so I'm looking Sirene in the eye. "What if I'm both?" My voice is strong.

A look of anger crosses Sirene's face, then vanishes. "I thought you would understand how I feel," she says. She tosses her hair over her shoulders. "I guess I was wrong."

"I guess so," I say. A sea turtle nudges my leg. I place my hand on its head. The turtle nudges me harder. "Look, I need to get back to my work."

"I'll leave you to it, then." Sirene doesn't wave as she swims away.

"That was weird," I mutter to the turtle, who is calmer now. "Let's see what we can do for you."

I'm finishing up with the last of the animals when Dana comes for a visit.

"Hey," she says, giving me a hug.

"Find any more animals?" I ask.

"We didn't see anything on the western side of Ice Canyon," she says. "We didn't get a chance to go east yet. Lulu went in that direction earlier."

"Are you going now?" I ask.

"Yep," Dana nods. "I told Nari I'd see how you were doing first."

"I'm done here for now. I'll come with you to look for more sea creatures," I say.

"Great!" Dana says.

We push through Dana's barrier of thicker waters and swim away from the empty pen. The ocean currents are refreshing once we are free. It feels good to move.

"What do you know about green mermaids?" I ask as we swim.

"Green mermaids? Why?" Dana asks. She slows down, and we come to a pause.

"Sirene came to see me today," I say.

"Sirene? What did she want?" Dana asks.

"I felt like she was trying to mess with me," I say. "She was trying to get me to feel sorry for her. She said she feels like she doesn't belong to the tribe because of her green skin."

Dana is shaking her head. Her red hair dances around her face. "Green mermaids have always been touchy," she says. "They claim they were the first mermaids. They say the rest of us descended from them."

"Is that true?" I ask.

Dana shrugs her round shoulders. "There's no such thing as the 'first' mermaid," she says. "But the green mermaids have always been vain."

"She said she got picked on because of her skin color," I say.

"I doubt that's true," Dana says. "Usually the green ones pick on the rest of us for not being green."

I remember Sirene's ice display. "She showed me how she can freeze water. Does she have any other powers?"

"I've never seen her display powers directly, so I can't say," Dana says. "But you know the stories about mermaids who lure sailors to their deaths? The ones who cause storms and shipwrecks?"

"Sure," I say. I've read some of those legends at the little library in town.

"Well, the green mermaids are the ones behind all of those stories," Dana tells me. "They are the ones who cause the most destruction. We have always been told to watch out for them."

"Are there lots of green mermaids left?" I ask.

"There aren't many mermaids left, period," Dana says. "I wonder why she was trying to make you feel bad for her."

"I have a few ideas," I say.

"Let's go find Lulu and Nari so we can all talk about it," Dana suggests.

"Good plan," I agree. Dana takes my hand, and we go find our friends. I am eager to tell them about my conversation with Sirene.

CHAPTER 7

"At least there aren't any more hurt sea creatures," Dana says. We searched for hours that afternoon but didn't find a single injured animal. While we were looking, I told them about what Sirene had said to me.

"I hope that whoever is harming the creatures is done," Nari says. She looks thoughtful as she takes a big bite of seaweed.

We are in the cave that the three of them share. I feel a surge of jealousy. I wish I could have my own apartment. My mermaid friends are lucky. Most mer stop living with their parents when they turn thirteen.

I won't be able to live on my own for at least four more years. Even better, the cave is on the outskirts of Ice Canyon, so it's really private.

"I doubt it," Lulu says. She shakes out her hair and starts combing it. I start doing the same with mine. I love how my hair doesn't get tangled in the water the way it does on land.

"What makes you say that?" Nari asks.

"Don't you feel like there has to be something more to it?" Lulu asks. "Why would someone or something hurt all the animals and then just be done with it?"

"What do you think is behind it?" I ask.

"I'm not sure," Lulu says. "But I don't think it's anything good." She puts down her comb and starts wrapping her hair in a scarf.

"What does your mom say?" I ask.

"She thinks it's a good sign that we didn't find more animals today. She hopes the problem goes away on its own," Lulu says.

"And?" I ask.

Lulu looks confused. "And what?"

"Even if it does stop, don't you want to find out who did it? Somebody needs to pay," I say.

All of my friends look confused now.

"If the injuries stop, it means whoever is behind it either had a change of heart or left the canyons," Dana explains. "That's punishment enough."

My arms flail through the air as I try to form an argument. I'm really worked up. "But it's not! If someone commits a crime, they need to pay."

"Is that how it works with humans?" Nari asks.

Her question silences me. Every once in awhile I say or do something that reminds me I'm not a full mermaid.

"Yeah. I guess it's not how it works here," I say.

"My mom is not just sitting around doing nothing," Lulu says. "She increased the number of guards around the canyon and sent some of them out to investigate. But they didn't find anything."

"I still wonder what 'X marks the spot' means," Dana says. She's squinting like she does when she's thinking through a problem.

"You think it means more than the cuts on the animals?" I ask.

"I don't know why, but I do. I feel like there has to be more to it," Dana says.

"I still think Sirene is involved somehow," I say.

"Maybe," Lulu says. "She said some weird things to you."

We float in silence for a few moments, thinking. Then Nari yawns so big her jaw pops.

"Well, we aren't going to solve anything more tonight," Nari says. "Good night."

"Good night," we say. We all start heading for our rooms too. The cave has one main room and several smaller chambers where we sleep.

I will never get used to sleeping in the water. Mermaids don't use beds or pillows. We mainly float in place. I never sleep well here.

I'm tired after doing all the healing, though. Maybe I will get good rest tonight. I swim to my room and try to make myself comfortable.

I've just fallen asleep when I hear a loud thunk on the roof of the cave. It sounds like someone dropped an anchor on the cave.

I hear another loud thud. I swim out of my room to find my friends huddled in a group in the main area.

"What was that?" I ask.

Nari is shivering. Dana puts her arms around her. In one hand Dana is holding a long stick that looks like a baseball bat.

"We don't know," Lulu says.

"It sounded like an anchor," I say.

"We're too far down for ships to anchor. Must have been something else," Lulu says.

"Maybe rocks? They break free of the canyon walls sometimes," Dana explains. She tightens her hold on Nari, who is still shaking. I realize that Dana really is holding a baseball bat.

"Where did you get the baseball bat?" I ask, distracted.

"Is that what it's called? I found it by the shore," Dana says.

Thud!

We flinch as something hits the roof again. Nari shakes even harder.

"Are you okay, Nari?" I ask.

"I'm just really scared," she says.

"Don't be afraid," Lulu says. "We should go check it out."

"No!" Nari says. "It's dark. You don't know what might be out there. What if it's the monster?"

"It's not a monster," Lulu says.

Just then, there is a horrible scraping sound on the roof of the cave. It sounds like a thousand zombies trying to scratch through the rocks.

"What's out there?" Nari shrieks.

THUD!

The roof of the cave shakes.

"Help!" Dana shouts.

"We're too far away! No one can hear us!" Lulu yells. For the first time, I regret that the cave is off by itself.

BOOM!

We scream again, clinging to each other.

"What was that?" I ask. We hold our breath, but there are no more sounds.

Then we hear a strange cry.

"You heard that too, right? That cry?" Dana asks. She sounds scared now, which makes me even more afraid.

We wait in silence for long minutes, holding on to each other. There are no more sounds.

"The roof may have been damaged," Lulu says eventually. "We have to go see." She scoops up one of the glowing jellyfish the mermaids use for light. She looks back at us. "Who's coming with me?"

I free myself from the group. "I will," I say. I try to sound brave.

"We'll wait for you here," Dana says. She presses her shoulder against Nari's.

I know Dana wants to go out with us, but I admire how she stays to take care of Nari.

Lulu nods, but I can see the fear in her eyes. Somehow knowing that Lulu is also afraid makes me feel better. She's facing her fears and going outside. I can do it too.

Holding the jellyfish high, we swim out of the cave. It's dark outside. The ocean is always dark to human eyes, at least this far underwater. During the day, I can see perfectly fine with my mer eyes. But at night, it's dark for everyone, mer and human.

Lulu takes my hand. I squeeze her fingers.

"Let's check out the roof first," Lulu says.

We swim up to the top of the cave. The whole time I'm waiting for something or someone to attack us. The jellyfish casts a weak circle of light around us. I don't see anyone except Lulu.

"The roof looks fine," she says. "We'll have to check again in the morning, but I don't see any major damage."

"Good. Let's go back inside," I say.

We're at the entrance to the cave when I see it. A tiny, lonely starfish lies on our doorstep.

Lulu sees it at the same time I do. "Is it okay?" she asks.

I reach out to touch the starfish. Even at first glance I can tell it's been badly hurt. "Let's get it inside," I say.

I scoop up the starfish and hold it close to my chest. When I lay it on the slab of rock that my friends use as a table, Dana, Nari, and Lulu crowd around.

One of the starfish's arms is dangling by a thread. Two arms were cut off entirely. Starfish can regrow limbs, but this one might be too damaged. A huge X marks its underside.

"We found it on the doorstep," Lulu explains. I barely hear her. I'm already busy trying to heal the poor creature.

"Can I help?" Nari asks. When I nod, her face goes soft. She's trying to communicate with the starfish.

"Anything?" I ask.

Tears well out of Nari's eyes. "The crying we heard was from the starfish," she says.

"I didn't know starfish made any sounds," I say, distracted. I'm still trying to heal the creature.

"They don't, normally. This one was being tortured," Nari says.

"Poor thing," Dana whispers.

I work on the starfish for hours. Longer than I've ever worked with any creature. In the end, it's not enough. The cuts are too deep. Sometime deep in the night, the starfish dies in my hands.

"Goodbye, little one," I murmur.

My friends are sleeping nearby. Nari wakes up and takes my hand. She leads me to my room and drapes a blanket of seaweed around my shoulders.

"Get some sleep," she says. "We'll figure it out in the morning."

"I couldn't save it," I say.

Nari squeezes my hand again. "You did your best," she says.

"It wasn't enough," I say. But Nari is already gone.

CHAPTER 8

"We have to do something!" Lulu says.

"We don't need to do anything," Dana reminds her.

"Yes, we do!" Lulu exclaims.

It is the morning after the starfish died in my hands. We are swimming to the *Clemmons* to see if we can learn anything more about the animal attacks. We disagree about our next steps. Lulu wants to charge ahead and find whoever or whatever is behind this. Nari thinks we should focus on finding and healing hurt animals.

"Your mother didn't ask us to go chasing after the monster," Nari reminds Lulu.

"So?" Lulu asks. "We can't just sit back and let sea creatures get hurt. Right, India?"

I actually agree with Lulu, but I don't want to get into a fight with my friends.

"We should do whatever we think is right," I say.

Lulu makes a face. "That's no help. What I think is right is not what Nari thinks is right."

"Maybe we should split up," I say. "Lulu and I can try to figure out what's behind the attacks. Dana and Nari can look for more animals."

"I suppose that could work," Dana agrees. "Although we'd need a way to find you if we have hurt animals."

"True," I say. "What if —"

My words are interrupted by something whizzing past my ear. For a second I thought it was a Frisbee, although I've never seen the mermaids play Frisbee.

I put my hand to my head. "What was that?"

A second bolt zooms past my head. Someone screams. "Look! Help!" They weren't Frisbees that flew past. They were harpoons.

I've seen harpoons in the museum where Grandpa works. They are long spears with sharp tips. They are used to hunt whales, seals, fish, and other creatures. But right now they are being used to hunt us.

We're all shouting as two merpeople appear out of nowhere. They are wearing capes with the hoods pulled low. Scarves are wrapped around their lower faces. I have no idea who they are. They must have been hiding behind a rock. At this point, it doesn't matter where they came from. What matters is that they are each holding a harpoon. And they are both swimming toward us.

"Run!" I shout, just as Lulu is shouting, "Swim!"

We take off swimming in the opposite direction. The water swirls around us. I'm a fast swimmer, but I'm not as fast as my mermaid friends.

Something grabs my ankle, and I give a huge kick. I look over my shoulder.

One of the hooded mermen is holding on to my foot. I'm reminded of all the times I've jumped into my bed at night, half convinced something would reach out from underneath the bed and grab my ankle.

I whimper and then find my voice. "Help!" I shout.

Lulu whirls around on her emerald green tail and holds up her hands. "Grab on to her!" she yells to Nari and Dana.

Nari clamps a hand around my wrist. Dana circles in a blur of pink and takes my other hand. With her other hand, she grabs on to a nearby rock ledge.

Lulu's face grows fierce. I watch as a wave rolls from her fingertips and comes crashing toward us. Nari and Dana tighten their hold on me.

The wave rolls over us. For several seconds, I am lost and confused. I don't know which way is up or down. All I know is that my friends are holding on to me.

I flutter my legs and kick. I can feel the moment when my ankle is free. Someone shouts, and the two hooded mermen are swept away.

"That should take care of them," Lulu says.

"Wow, that was really powerful," Nari says. She brushes her hair out of her eyes.

Dana is also looking at Lulu with respect. "I didn't know your gifts were getting to be so strong," she says.

Lulu looks at me. "They are when my friends are in danger."

My arms are shaking as I hug her. "Thanks."

"Of course," she says into my hair.

We all hold hands and start swimming in the direction of the *Clemmons*.

"Who were they?" Nari asks. We look over our shoulders to make sure we are not still being followed.

"No idea," Lulu says. Her curls bounce in the water. "I couldn't get a good look at their faces."

"They threw harpoons at us," I say. I'm still in shock about it.

"This is getting scary," Nari says. "Even when the Ice Canyon and Fire Canyon mer disagree, no one throws harpoons."

"Who threw harpoons?" someone asks from behind us. We all jump until we realize it's Evan.

"Two merpeople just came out of nowhere and started throwing harpoons at us," I say. The words burst out of me.

Evan looks horrified. His eyes are wide. He swims a few inches closer to me. "They did? India, are you okay?"

"Yeah, I'm fine," I say.

"How's everyone else?" Evan asks, looking at my friends.

"Nobody got hurt," Nari says.

"Did you see who it was?" Evan asks.

"None of us did," I say. "They came out of nowhere."

"Wait, where did you come from just now?" Lulu demands. Her voice is stern. She throws her arm out to block the rest of us from moving forward.

Evan looks surprised. "I was just on my way from the *Clemmons*."

"Uh-huh," Lulu says.

His eyes get even wider. "You don't think I had anything to do with this, do you?"

"Hard to say," Lulu says. She looks him up and down. "The mer who attacked us were wearing hoods. We couldn't see their faces. It could have been anyone."

I've heard enough. "Lulu, you can't really think that Evan is involved, can you?" I say.

"I'm looking at all the options," she says, folding her arms across her chest.

"Lulu, this is silly," I say.

"Why can't he be involved?" she asks. "Just because you have a crush on him doesn't mean he's not involved."

There's a certain kind of coral near Ice Canyon that is bright red. I'm pretty sure my cheeks are the same color right now.

"Lulu. Enough," Dana says.

Lulu twirls to face Dana. "Evan could be involved," she says. "He's the first person we saw after the attack. I'm not saying it is him, but it's a possibility. Right?"

"Dana, you know that's not right!" I protest.

Dana squints. "You have to admit it is a possibility, India," she says. She turns to Evan. "I don't think you're involved, Evan. But it's possible."

"It's not possible," Evan says.

"Anything is possible," Lulu counters.

I throw up my hands. "I can't believe I'm hearing this!" I cry. "You can't just go around accusing people of crimes they didn't commit."

"And you can't let your feelings for people cloud your thoughts," Lulu says. She lays her hands on my shoulders.

I squirm away from her. "You're being unfair. And unreasonable." I look at Dana. "So are you."

"I'm just trying to keep us safe," Lulu says.

I might have forgiven her if she looked sorry. Instead she looked pleased with herself.

"You're only saying this because you're always trying so hard to impress your mother," I say. "You want to be the one to solve the mystery and win her attention."

As soon as I say it, I regret it. It's a low blow. I know it. Everyone else knows it too. Dana shakes her head. Nari gasps. I can't even look at Evan.

Lulu grits her teeth and exhales a long stream of water. "Well, it's good to know how you feel, India Finch. Good luck with your work." She swims away, her tail moving slowly up and down.

"Someone should go after her," Nari says.

"I'll go," Dana offers.

"I'm sorry. I shouldn't have said that," I say.

Evan replies, "Everyone's stressed."

Dana's eyes are sad. "You should apologize to Lulu in person, India. We'll see you later." She gives Nari's hand a squeeze and swims after Lulu.

"I messed things up," I murmur. I'm ashamed. I said a terrible thing to my friend. But she shouldn't have accused Evan of being involved.

"We should go," Nari says. Her hand is cool on my arm. Evan floats a few feet away, looking uncomfortable.

"Just give me a minute," I say.

CHAPTER 9

I leave Evan and Nari and swim around a corner. I need a tiny pity party. I find a shallow cave, duck inside, and let the tears come. The salt from my tears mixes with the salt from the ocean. The sensation is oddly comforting.

I cry until I'm done.

"Finished feeling sorry for yourself?" Nari asks. I see her hovering at the mouth of the cave. Evan is a few feet behind her.

I laugh in spite of myself. "Yes, I guess I am. I want to find Lulu and say I'm sorry."

"Yes, but first you need to hear what Evan found," Nari says.

I give Evan a weak smile. "I'm sorry. About everything back there."

"It's okay," Evan says.

A thought occurs to me. "Why aren't the Fire Canyon mer more worried? I don't see any of them looking for hurt sea creatures. If the dome dissolves, it affects them too."

Evan looks miserable as he speaks. "I think my dad hopes that if the dome disappears, he'd have an excuse to start a war with the humans."

I feel like I've been punched in the stomach. I knew Fire Canyon wanted to attack humans, but a part of me assumed they were all talk and no action.

"How?" I ask.

"Huh?" Evan asks.

"How would he start a war?" I ask.

"He talks about stirring up huge storms and cutting the transatlantic cables. That kind of thing," Evan says.

"Cutting the cables would cause problems with communication," I say, nodding.

"At least for a while," Evan says. "But it's a losing battle. There are too many humans and not enough mer. We would never win."

"Do you want to go to war?" Nari asks.

Evan shakes his head. He answers Nari's question, but he keeps his eyes on me. "I want the oceans to be clean again," he says. "But I don't want to hurt humans."

The silence stretches between us. Finally Nari nudges Evan. "Tell India what you told me," she says.

"Oh, right," Evan says. "I want you to know that I wasn't involved in the harpoon thing earlier."

"I know," I say.

"I only came to find you because I think I know what 'X marks the spot' means," Evan says.

"You do? What is it?" I ask.

"Let me show you," he says.

Evan leads us to the *Clemmons*. A few mer are hanging out at the ship already, but no one I know well. A lot of the mer are still sleeping.

"I don't see Lulu or Dana," Nari says. She stops in the water to look at the shipwreck.

"Maybe they went to talk to Ani," I say. "We'll find them soon."

"Let's keep going," Evan says.

We're about to swim away when a figure pulls away from the shipwreck. A mermaid swims toward us. The sunlight in the water shines on her blond hair.

It's Melody. My heart sinks.

"Hi, Evan," she calls as she slides through the water. Even her swimming is perfect.

"Hey, Melody," he says.

"And you've got Nari and India with you," Melody says. She stops in front of us. Her ice-blue tail glitters.

"Nice to see you, Melody," Nari says. She's always polite.

I just glare at Melody. Not that it matters. She doesn't even look in my direction.

"You're coming to the feast tonight, aren't you?" Melody asks Evan. "I'll save a seat for you."

"Um, sure," Evan says. "But you'd better save seats for Nari and India too."

"And for Lulu and Dana," Nari pipes up. "Thanks, Melody."

We swim away before Melody can answer. She has a sour look on her face.

"What dinner?" I ask.

"One of the gatherings that Ani and Storm have for both tribes," Nari explains.

"Oh, those," I say. Lulu told me that Ani and Storm have hosted dinners for a few years. All of the mer from both tribes are supposed to go. The feasts take place at the clearing between the canyons, the biggest spot to fit three hundred mer. "How are those going?"

"They're okay," Nari answers. "There weren't any fights the last time."

"That's something," I say.

When I heard about the dinners on my first trip to the canyons, I asked Lulu why Ani and Storm insist on having them. The tribes don't like each other. Surely they don't want to eat together.

But Lulu said that the mer know they have to find a way to get along.

The mer have been lucky that the dome covers both tribes, even though the tribes themselves don't live in harmony with each other. No one can risk the dome breaking down because of the tribes. The dinners help.

"Where did you say we were going?" I ask Evan.

"I guess I'm going to the dinner tonight," he mumbles. "But I hope you go with me."

I nearly stop swimming. "Yeah, sure," I say. "I'd love to go to the dinner with you."

"You would?" Evan says. His face breaks into a bright smile.

"Yes," I say. "But I was asking where we're going now."

"Oh," he says. He blushes. "Sorry."

"No problem," I say. I glance at Nari, who is trying very hard not to laugh.

"Just over here," Evan says.

We are out of sight of the *Clemmons*. Melody hasn't followed us. It's just the three of us.

Evan leads us around a corner, and I realize where we are. Huge cliffs tower above us, twice as tall as the cliffs at Ice Canyon. The currents are fast here, spinning past jagged rock.

"We're not supposed to be here," Nari says. She swims a few feet behind us.

"This is the Breakers, isn't it?" I ask.

"It's off limits to Ice Canyon mer," Nari says. "The currents are so strong that even the best swimmers get swept away and crash into the rocks."

"The Breakers are off limits to Fire Canyon too," Evan answers. "But look."

He points at the edge of a cliff. Two rocks have fallen against each other. The boulders are taller than me. They are thin and jagged. And the way they have fallen forms an X.

"X marks the spot," I whisper.

I start to swim toward the rocks.

"Wait!" Evan shouts behind me.

I barely hear him as my feet get swept away. Suddenly I'm tumbling head over heels. I reach out, but there's nothing to grab on to.

My hand slams against a rock. My leg hits another rock. I feel a moment of terror. I'm going to be smashed in the canyon.

I start kicking as hard as I can. I gulp, swallowing water. I start coughing. Suddenly I can't see. Where are Evan and Nari?

My arms flail, and my chest is burning.

Swim, India.

"Mom?"

Swim. This time the voice sounds like Grandpa. I sob. The water churns around me. For the first time, I wonder if I'm going to die here.

Then strong hands grab my arms.

"Hold on!" Evan shouts. He starts pulling me out of the currents.

The ocean does not want to let me go, but Evan is stronger. He pulls me into calmer water. I fall into Nari's arms. Evan's arms close around both of us.

"I've got you," Evan says, his voice a low murmur.

"I've got you too," Nari whispers.

Tears form in the corner of my eyes. I can't believe I got caught in the current. What would have happened to me if Evan and Nari hadn't been there?

"I guess I know why the Breakers are off limits," I mumble.

"Yeah," Nari says with a weak laugh.

"Why did you do that?" Evan asks.

I shrug and his arms fall away. "I was trying to get closer to the X."

Evan's face looks bleak. "I didn't mean for you to swim into it," he says. "I wanted to show you where it was. Then we could come back with seaweed ropes and about twenty other mer to help."

"Oh," I say. "Well, next time let me know the plan before I go charging in."

I'm trying to make Evan laugh or at least smile. It works. He grins and brushes a lock of hair from my face. I lean toward him slightly and notice when he starts to lean toward me.

"You're bleeding," Nari says, interrupting us.

I look at my arm, where there's a big cut. My leg is also scratched up.

"I can fix it," I say.

Nari and Evan lead me to a quiet cave. I take a few deep breaths to settle my nerves. Then I summon the healing power of water. I move my free hand over my arm. I fix the gash and then turn my focus to the smaller cuts on my leg.

"Better," I say when I'm done.

"I'll never get tired of seeing you do that," Evan says.

"What do we think about the X?" Nari asks.

"It seems like the best clue we've got," I say. "Let's come back and check it out further. We should go tell the others."

"Exactly. And you have a few apologies to make," Nari says. She takes my hand and we swim away from the Breakers, Evan swimming next to us. I'm anxious to see Lulu and Dana now. What would have happened if I'd died and never got a chance to say I'm sorry?

CHAPTER 10

As dinner comes to a close that night I lean against a smooth rock. The sea is dark above and around us. Jellyfish glow around the circle. Their light is soft, like candles.

My belly is full. Dinner was good, even if it was mainly seaweed. The seaweed never tastes like much to me but it fills me up. Thankfully, I lose my human appetite in the waters, especially since there's no way to pack a bunch of peanut butter and banana sandwiches.

I look overhead, wishing I could see the stars. Even on a clear night, you can't see the stars from the bottom of the sea.

I try to pretend the glowing jellyfish are stars, but it doesn't work. I guess it doesn't matter. The night is still magical.

Lulu is next to me. Dana sits near Lulu's tail. Nari is on my other side. Evan hovers nearby. He has been sitting with us the entire night. Melody sits across the circle with the Fire Canyon mer. She looks mad, but less mad than how Lulu looked when I first found her this evening.

I had apologized the instant I saw her. "I'm so sorry. It was a terrible thing to say. And I'm a horrible friend. And I was angry. And I love you so much!"

It wasn't a graceful apology, but it was heartfelt. Lulu took one look at my sobbing face and started to cry too.

"It's okay!" she had said. "I love you too."

Then we linked arms and pounced on the seaweed buffet. Later Nari, Evan, and I told Lulu and Dana about the Breakers. They gasped at all the right places and agreed to go check it out in the morning when it is light.

"I really am sorry about what I said," I tell Lulu, thinking back on my first apology.

She grins and shakes her head. "I already told you, it's fine," she says. "Besides, I said some bad things too."

"What you said was upsetting," I admit. "But I there's some truth to it."

"What do you mean?" Lulu asks.

"I did let my feelings about Evan cloud my thinking," I say. "I like him. I don't want to think anything bad about him."

"We all know you like him," Lulu says. "I wasn't surprised you took his side."

"But I don't know him as well as I know you. I should have trusted you. I guess it was possible Evan was involved," I say.

"No, it wasn't," Lulu says. "Evan may be from another tribe, but I've known him most of my life. He's a good guy."

"Why did you say he might be involved?" I ask, confused.

Lulu picks at the scraps of seaweed on her plate. "You were right too. I was trying to impress my mom. So I started saying things I didn't really believe."

"She's your mom. She loves you so much. I don't get why you think you need to impress her," I say.

Lulu nods her head to the middle of the circle. Ani and Storm are sitting together. Their heads are close. They are having an intense conversation. Besides our group, they are the only Ice Canyon and Fire Canyon members sitting together.

"I know my mom loves me. And she is proud that I'm so independent. But sometimes . . ." Her voice trails off.

"Sometimes parents get wrapped up in their own drama and forget about their kids," I finish. I don't say it, but I'm thinking about my own parents. How could they just send me away for the entire summer? The question opens a hole in my heart.

"Yeah," Lulu says. "Sometimes I feel overlooked."

"I haven't forgotten you," I say. I give her a hug. "I won't ever forget you."

"Neither will I," Dana says. She sounds sleepy.

"Me neither," Nari says.

We settle in to listen to the stories. An Ice Canyon mermaid is telling a story about three mermaids who sang beautiful songs long ago. Sailors would steer their ships toward the sound. The mermaids thought the sailors' ships were getting too close to where the mermaids lived. They started singing near dangerous rocks to lure the sailors into danger. It worked. The ships got caught on the rocks and sank.

"That's uplifting," I comment.

"They were just protecting their home," Lulu says. "Wouldn't you do the same?"

I think about my house in Ohio. It's not fancy or old or huge. But it's my house, where I grew up.

"I don't know," I say. "I'll be sad when I leave for college in a few years. And I'll be sad if my parents sell our house." *Or split up*, I think. "But I don't know if I'd try to protect it at all costs."

"What about this home?" Nari asks, her voice light. "Would you protect this home?"

I look around the circle. A school of tuna swims past. The light from the jellyfish makes the coral glow like Christmas lights. My friends told me the dome is a soft rose color, faint but visible. The danger seems like it has passed.

The Fire Canyon mer and the Ice Canyon mer sit on opposite sides of the circle. People look at each other with suspicion. But no one is fighting. The tribes do not like each other, but they are still here. I realize they are doing what they can to protect their home.

I also realize I would do whatever it takes to protect this place.

"I would help," I start to say. "Whatever it took —"

My words are interrupted by a harsh laugh. For a second I think it is one of my friends before I realize the sound is coming from the middle of the circle.

"What a truly pathetic story," a voice is saying.

"Sirene?" Ani says. "What are you doing?"

Sirene is floating in the middle of the circle. Her hair is a wild tangle around her face. Her tail beats a slow, steady pulse.

"I didn't know she was here," Lulu whispers to me.

"She just got here," Dana says.

"I'm revising the story," Sirene is saying to everyone.

"What are you talking about?" Ani says. Storm is floating next to her. He looks worried.

"Those mermaids didn't cause shipwrecks to protect their home," she says. "They caused the shipwrecks to punish the sailors."

I sit up. The feeling around the circle has changed. Before, there was a sense of rest and relaxation. Now it feels like a fight might break out after all.

"The mer don't need tricks to protect their homes," Sirene says. "We are more powerful than all the humans! This is not new information."

I see that most of the Fire Canyon mer are nodding their heads. Many of the Ice Canyon mer are doing the same.

"We huddle here in the canyons. We have our disagreements. This is not right," Sirene says. "Someone was hurting the sea creatures. The ocean waters are dirty. Our homes are being destroyed."

I look around the circle again. Many of the mer are starting to clap. They are rising from their resting places as Sirene keeps talking.

"We must band together. No more of this Ice Canyon or Fire Canyon separation. We must come together as one tribe. Now is the time. Now is the time to fight back. Now is the time to punish the humans and take back our ocean!" she shouts.

There is a roar of approval. I start to edge back from the circle. I'm part-mer, but I'm afraid they will only see my human features.

"We should leave," Evan whispers in my ear.

"I think that's a good idea," Dana says. Lulu and Nari are already forming a screen in front of me. I'm afraid, but I'm also so thankful for my friends right now.

"Enough!" Ani's voice cuts through the circle.

I can see why she's the leader. Her voice is powerful. The clapping dies down.

"We will not be attacking anyone tonight," Ani says. "That is not the way of the mer."

"It's the way of the Fire Canyon mer!" someone shouts. The crowd murmurs. For a second I think Ani has lost control. Sirene looks smug.

"If you agree with me, follow me!" Sirene says. Mer start moving toward her.

"Not tonight." Storm's voice rumbles through the crowd. Everyone freezes. I notice that he and Ani are holding hands.

"We will not be attacking anyone," Storm says. "On this, Ani and I agree."

"No good comes from us attacking the humans," Ani says. "There are many reasons why we should not fight them. But the biggest is that if we fight them, they will know we exist. And if they know we exist, they will never leave us in peace."

"Go home," Storm commands. "This is not the time for war."

Many of the mer look upset and angry, but everyone leaves. The Fire Canyon mer shoot Storm dirty looks.

Sirene watches them leave. Then she shrugs her shoulders and swims away. Ani drops Storm's hand and swims away.

"She has to be dealt with, Ani," Storm calls after her. "And soon."

"I know," she says.

Ani swims over to us and gives Lulu a hug. She sees Evan. "You should go."

Evan sighs. "I don't agree with Sirene."

Ani lays her hand on Evan's cheek. The gesture surprises me. "I know you don't. Still, it's best if you go home with your dad."

Evan gives me a crooked smile. "See you tomorrow?" he asks.

"Sure. Tomorrow," I say. I try not to sigh as he swims away.

"India, I want you and the girls to stay in my cave tonight," Ani says. "Tomorrow I'll send you back to your grandfather. It's not safe for you here."

"I want to stay," I say. "What if you have more injured animals?"

"We'll figure that out," Ani says. "We haven't had any in a few days. Maybe the monster is gone."

"But what about the dead starfish? And the mer who followed us?" I ask. I know Lulu and Dana told Ani about the attacks. Ani was horrified by the news. She increased the number of guards in Ice Canyon immediately. But no one has caught the attackers.

"All the more reason to send you home," she says.

"What if the mer who attacked us were Fire Canyon mer? Won't Evan be in danger too? And the rest of Fire Canyon?" I protest.

"Storm knows about the attacks," Ani says.

"He does?" I ask. "What did he say about them?"

Ani levels me with her stare. "He denies them, of course. And he's looking into it."

"And you trust him?" I ask. It's the wrong thing to say.

"I trust Storm," Ani says. "Now let's go."

I can tell by the tone of Ani's voice that it is no use arguing. I glance back at Evan, who is swimming away with his dad. He sees me looking and gives one last wave. As I follow Ani and my friends, I wonder if I'll ever see Evan again.

CHAPTER 11

The next morning Ani shakes me awake.

"Are you sending me back already?" I mumble. I am still half asleep. I am not going to let her send me back, however. I will stay and help.

"I should," Ani says.

I open my eyes fully. "But you're not?" I ask.

Ani shakes her head. "Not right now. Even though I want to. Come with me. You need to see something."

Ani leads me to the entrance of the cave. I let out a cry when I see them.

Dozens of fish, a few turtles, several lobsters, two seals. All of them are hurt. Their blood trickles through the water.

"The dome is weakening," Ani says. "Someone is sending us a message."

"Who would do this?" Lulu asks. She, Dana, and Nari appear behind us. Nari gasps and takes Dana's hand.

"I don't know," Ani says, shaking her head. "But we're going to stop it."

I spend the morning healing the sea creatures. About half of them die this time, their wounds too deep for me to heal. I'm torn up by the deaths, no matter how many times Nari tells me I've done all that I can.

"Let's go meet Lulu and Dana at the *Clemmons*," is all I say.

Evan is waiting for us at the ship.

"What are you doing here?" I sputter.

"I heard about the sea creatures," Evan says. "You can almost see through the dome near Fire Canyon."

"It's the same at Ice Canyon," Lulu says.

"My fault," I whisper. Sorrow and guilt crash over me like one of Lulu's waves.

My friends look at me like I'm crazy.

"The injuries were worse than before," I say. "Almost half of the sea creatures died this morning." My voice is hoarse.

Everyone moves toward me as if to hug me, but Lulu gets to me first. She grips my shoulders and looks into my face.

"If you hadn't been here, they all would have died. Place blame where it belongs. It's not your fault. Do you believe me?" she asks.

A knot of guilt releases inside of me. I'm deeply sad that the creatures died, but Lulu's right. I can't blame myself.

"I do believe you," I say. "So let's find out who is to blame."

"The Breakers?" Lulu asks.

"The Breakers," I confirm.

"Good. I'm going with you," Evan says, and we all set off.

I know we are getting close when the currents get stronger. I get caught in a small wave and bump against Evan. He takes my hand to steady me. Our fingers clasp. Neither of us lets go.

Once we reach the Breakers, we all hang back to let Lulu work. She spends several minutes studying the flow of water. She tries a few different things to redirect the currents. Eventually she figures out a way to slow the water.

"Done!" she calls over her shoulder. Her arms are lifted high. The water churns on her left and her right. In front of her, the water is still.

"Would you look at that," Dana says. She tilts her head to one side. Lulu stilled the water right in front of the rocks that made an X. Beyond the rocks is a passageway.

"A secret tunnel," Nari whispers.

"If you're going to go, you'd better do it now!" Lulu shouts. "I can't hold this for much longer."

"Go!" someone yells. We tumble past Lulu into the mouth of the tunnel. Lulu follows us. Then we hear a crashing sound as the currents resume their normal pattern.

"Will we be able to get back out again?" Evan asks.

"Of course we will," Nari replies. "We have Lulu."

The tunnel is dark as we creep down it. Evan is still holding my hand. I bump into Dana, who is in front of me.

"Oops! Sorry," I say.

"You're swimming on my fin," someone else says in the darkness.

There is another round of apologies.

"Wait, I forgot," Nari says. The inside of the tunnel is filled suddenly with a soft glow. "I knew I brought this for a reason."

Nari is holding a tiny glowing jellyfish in her palm. We can now see where we are going.

"Good thinking," Dana says.

"Look," Lulu says.

She point at the side of the tunnel. Strange carvings line the walls.

"What is it?" Evan asks.

"I don't know," I say. I edge forward to read the carvings since the mermaids do not have a written language. "Looks like something from an Egyptian pyramid."

"What do you think it means?" Nari asks.

"Hard to say," Dana answers. "We don't know who carved this or when. We don't even know if this is related to the hurt sea creatures."

"It gives me the creeps," Evan comments.

"We should keep going," I say.

We are halfway down the tunnel when a large tuna comes swimming toward us. Its fin is injured, causing it to swim lopsidedly.

"Hey, it's okay," I croon to the fish, which flinches.

Nari moves closer and closes her eyes. I can tell she is communicating with the tuna. The fish relaxes and lets me touch it. I fix its fin first. Then I heal the X that has been carved above its gills.

"I guess we're in the right place," Evan comments as I let the fish go.

"Can it get through the currents?" I ask.

"It should be fine," Lulu replies.

We keep creeping down the passage. The tunnel is long. I am on the lookout for more injured sea creatures.

An eel comes toward us. It brushes my leg and sends a shiver down my spine. I pause to heal the X on its neck.

We are almost at the end of the tunnel. A greenish light glows ahead of us.

"I guess this is it," Lulu says as we reach the end of the tunnel.

Suddenly I realize how unprepared we are. The mermaids all have powers, but none of us have harpoons or spears. We didn't even let anyone know where we were going. We should have at least told Ani what our plans were. Although I suppose she would have forbidden us from coming.

"Does your dad know where you are?" I ask Evan.

He shakes his head. "He wouldn't have let me come," he says. "He would have said it was too dangerous."

"Yeah, I'm starting to get that," I say.

"What should we do?" Lulu asks.

I'm nervous that she sounds uncertain. I guess we are all getting cold feet. Or cold fins, as the case may be.

"We came this far," Nari says.

In the end, there's nothing left to do but hold hands and swim into the greenish light.

CHAPTER 12

There is nothing special about the room at the end of the tunnel, except for the fact that it is bathed in green light. The walls are mostly smooth. A few rocks are scattered across the sand floor. The entire space is smaller than Ani's cave.

A stone the size of a kitchen table sits in the middle. A spiny sea urchin moves sluggishly on the rock. Behind the stone is Sirene.

Her hair floats in a dark mass behind her head. She smiles lazily. She does not look surprised to see us.

"You," I say. I'm not surprised to see her, either.

"I was wondering if you'd find me," she says. Then she flutters her fingers and cuts the urchin with blades of ice.

We leap into motion. Lulu starts generating currents. Dana thickens the water around Sirene. Nari and I move toward the sea urchin.

But Sirene is too fast for us. She puts up her hands. Suddenly we are all thrown backward, like we hit an invisible wall.

"No so fast," Sirene says.

"What was that?" Lulu whispers. She rubs her head where she hit the wall.

"Those were my powers," Sirene laughs. Her laughter is dark and cruel.

Two mer stand guard at the opening. A mermaid and a merman. They grip their harpoons tight. We must have passed right by them when we came into the cave. I recognize the merman — Storm's friend Poe. The one who looks like a football player. I don't recognize the other one.

Evan sees them too. "Poe?" he asks. He looks at the other guard. "And Kate?"

The guards frown.

"Does my father know you're here?" Evan asks.

"This doesn't concern Storm," Poe says.

I can see the relief on Evan's face. "Why are you here, then?" he asks.

"We believe in Sirene," Kate says. Her green eyes glitter in the shadows of the cave.

"What does that even mean?" I ask.

Sirene laughs behind us, the sound low and creepy. "They believe in my vision," she says.

"And what vision is that?" I demand.

The sea urchin shakes on the rock.

"It's hurt," Nari says. She swims close to the rock and holds out a hand. Sirene watches her.

"Yes, it is," Sirene gloats.

"Why do you hurt them?" Nari asks. "Are you trying to destroy the dome?"

"Of course I am, my dear girl," Sirene says.

She flings her arms wide open and continues. "Destroying that silly bubble ends the world that we have. It ushers in a new age!" I sense the mood in the cave shift. Sirene looks giddy.

"We want to hear your plans, Sirene," I say. "But first will you let me heal the sea urchin?"

Sirene tilts her head, considering me. She holds my gaze for a long time. For a second I think she'll let me do it.

"No," she says at last. Then she starts to laugh. "Why would I let you heal the urchin? The dome won't get weaker if you keep healing the animals."

I am looking around at everything, trying to come up with a plan. I can't think of anything. I look at my friends. I don't know if they have thought up a plan either. They all look scared and confused.

Lulu catches my eye. She shrugs her shoulders and shakes her head. We need to keep Sirene talking. If nothing else, it will buy us time.

"So, um, tell me about this new age you're trying to create," I say.

I try to sound casual, like we are two friends meeting at a coffee shop. I'm glad we're in water, and Sirene can't hear my knees shaking together.

Sirene laughs, low and dark. "Do you really not know?"

"Um," I say, "no, that's why I'm asking."

Sirene swims over to me. Her tail swishes through the water. I float in place. I won't let her see that I'm scared.

"What is the mer's biggest problem?" she asks.

I want to tell her that I think she is the mer's biggest problem, but I don't think she would like that.

"Well, humans, I guess," I say.

"And why do you say that?" she asks.

"Humans have polluted the oceans and destroyed many mermaid habitats," I say. Shame wells in me.

"Yes," Sirene says. "Humans have done these things. And the mer must fight back." She swirls around the cave, returning to the table. She looks at all of us. "But there is an even bigger problem."

"What is it?" Lulu asks. Her voice sounds hoarse.

"This," Sirene says, gesturing to us.

"What do you mean?" I ask. "Us being friends? Do you mean me?"

"Not everything centers on you," Sirene sniffs. "No, I'm talking about the divide between the tribes." She points to us again.

I notice that Evan floats a few yards away from my friends. I give him a look. He barely meets my eyes. But I can see that he's edging closer to the Fire Canyon guards.

Is Evan leaving us? Is he siding with the Fire Canyon mer? Or does he have a plan? I push aside my worry and focus on Sirene.

"If the tribes cannot unite, we will never defeat humans," Sirene says. "It is that simple."

"That doesn't make any sense," Dana says. "The Ice Canyon mer aren't interested in defeating humans. Even if the tribes unite, you will never convince the Ice Canyon tribe to turn against humans."

"Oh, but I can," Sirene says. "I almost already have."

"What are you talking about?" Lulu asks.

"I'm talking about last night," Sirene says. "You were there. You saw how the tribes supported me. You saw how the mer were willing to join me."

"Those were empty words," I say.

"Were they?" Sirene asks. "I'm not so sure. They know something is hurting the sea creatures. They might not believe humans are behind it. But it will not take much more to convince them that humans are the cause of most of their problems."

"Humans haven't been hurting the sea creatures, though," Nari says. She and Dana are floating next to each other. "You have."

"The tribes will never know that," Sirene says. "The bubble will fade, and the canyons will be exposed." Sirene shrugs. "Everyone will unite behind me. I will provide the kind of leadership they need."

"My mother will never allow it," Lulu says. "Neither will Evan's dad."

"Too late," Sirene says. "They will never know until it's too late to stop us."

I realize then that Sirene is not planning to let us go. She's going to kill us.

"What are you going to do to the humans?" I ask. Time is running out. I don't have a plan. I have to keep Sirene talking.

"We have to get the humans to make the first move, of course," Sirene says. "Once the bubble vanishes, we will lure humans here with a mermaid sighting. Then we will attack."

"Attack how?" I ask. My voice wavers.

"It will be glorious!" Sirene says. "We will kill those who come to this place. Then we will send tidal waves to flood the coastal towns and sink any ship that tries to come near us."

"Sounds complex," I comment. I am only half listening to Sirene's rambles. I've been looking for a way to escape. Our only hope is to blast our way past the guards.

I look closer at the guards. I realize where I've seen them before, in addition to the time I saw them with Storm. "You had them attack us," I say.

My comment draws everyone's attention to the door. As we move, I catch my friends' eyes. I hope they understand what I'm trying to tell them.

"Yes," Sirene says.

"They threw harpoons at us," I say. "They almost killed us."

"Yes," Sirene says again.

"I don't understand. Why try to kill us then? We didn't know much," I say, turning back to her.

"You were getting in my way," she says. "I tried to warn you. You wouldn't listen."

Another puzzle piece falls into place. "You left the starfish for us," I say.

"I did," Sirene confirms. "You were supposed to be so scared that you left. It's not my fault you didn't."

"No," I say, remembering what Lulu told me about blame. "It's your fault you got us into this mess in the first place."

Sirene looks confused.

I make my voice loud. I puff out my chest. "NOW!" I shout.

CHAPTER 13

The instant I shout, the cave erupts. Lulu and Dana unleash their powers. Currents sweep past us and back again. The water around me thickens and thins. I can barely see anything in the swirling water.

Sirene shrieks and lifts her hands. Bolts of ice sail past my head from the left. I duck.

"You will not get away with this!" Sirene shouts.

Lulu and Dana are creating a storm within the cave. It is almost like being trapped inside a snow globe. As particles of sand race past my face, I realize it is exactly like being trapped inside a snow globe.

"India!" Evan shouts. I make my way toward the sound of his voice. He is at the entrance to the cave, wrestling Poe. Evan really is on our side.

I reach the entrance and begin to tear at Poe's arms, trying to pull him away from Evan. Evan is almost half Poe's size, but he did not hesitate to fight the bigger man.

"Behind you!" Evan shouts. I duck as another bolt of ice flies past my ears. Sirene comes at me, but she is knocked into the side of the cave by one of Lulu's currents. Dana cheers. We are winning!

"Let's get out of here!" I shout. I make my way to the entrance. Nari is behind me. Dana and Lulu are on the other side of the cave. Dana is thickening the water around Sirene. She will be trapped long enough for us to escape.

"Let's go!" I shout again. Then a hand clamps over my wrists and draws my arms behind my back.

"Not so fast," a voice says in my ear. Kate, the other guard, has captured me.

I struggle against Kate's hands. She does not budge an inch.

"It's no use," she says. "I'm too strong."

It's true. Kate is stronger than a bodybuilder. Her strength must be her mermaid power. Kate turns me to face Sirene. Around me, my friends have stopped fighting.

"Well, then," Sirene says, straightening her shirt and smoothing her hair. She has slid free from Dana's water barrier.

"What are you going to do to us?" I ask.

Sirene's smile is like a knife. "Wrong question." She raises her hand against me.

I see it in her eyes. She's going to kill us.

"Wait," I say. "Not like this. At least let me have my hands free."

Sirene considers my request. "I suppose it can't hurt. You can't hurt me. I'm too strong." She nods over my shoulder to Kate. My hands are freed.

I look at Sirene's face. She is beautiful, it's true. I can see why the green mermaids were so dangerous, how they lured sailors to their deaths. I understand why people would be tempted to follow her now.

I look closer. I start to see other things. I see bitterness in her eyes. I see that the bitterness masks something else — loneliness.

Deep down Sirene is lonely. She has spent so much time on her own. She misses her kind. A part of her is sad and scared. Just like everyone else.

A feeling rises in me. Not love. But it is something similar. I don't like what Sirene is doing. I don't want her to hurt me or my friends. But I also feel sorry for her. She is trapped by her sadness.

Without really knowing what I'm doing, I raise my hands. I call on my healing powers, letting them flow down my fingertips and into Sirene.

"What are you doing?" she gasps as my powers touch her. She stares at me.

"You don't have to be alone anymore," I say. I continue to send healing powers toward her. "You don't have to do this. You can choose another way."

Sirene looks horrified. She is angry. But beneath the anger I see something else. Hope?

I will never know.

Sirene's face changes. She snarls as she lunges at me. "Do not try to heal me, you foolish girl!" she snaps. She raises her hand. Bolts of ice scrape my cheek.

"Hold her!" she commands. Kate reaches for my hands. I know that the next time Sirene sends bolts of ice at me, she will plunge them straight into my heart.

At that moment, my ears catch the sound of a distant rumble. For a second I think there's a thunderstorm. Then I remember we're underwater.

"Sirene," Poe says, trying to get her attention.

"Be quiet!" she screams.

"But I think you should see this —"

Poe's words are interrupted by a flood of sea creatures spilling through the entrance to the cave. Seals and tuna, cod and lobster, followed by sea turtles and starfish. I see countless jellyfish and sea urchins. There is even a small spiny dogfish shark.

Sirene screams as the creatures surround her. She raises her arms and tries sending bolts of ice at them. I brace myself for the carnage but something is different.

"What's happening?" Sirene cries.

"She lost her powers," Lulu says, amazed. We watch as nothing but water streams from Sirene's fingertips.

"You must have melted her ice powers somehow," Dana says.

"How did I do that?" I wonder, but I see that something changed when I tried to heal her. She can't produce the ice bolts that were the core of her powers.

"Don't let them hurt me!" Sirene begs.

The creatures hover in a ring around her. I see more of them in the passageway.

"Nari?" Dana says. "Maybe we should move this party outside."

"What? Oh," Nari says. She closes her eyes. Suddenly the circle of sea creatures begins to move. A second ring forms around Poe and Kate.

"Did you do this?" I ask Nari.

"Did I summon the creatures who were hurt by Sirene so they can confront her?" Nari asks. "Yeah, I did."

A burst of warmth fills my chest.

"Don't hurt me. Please don't hurt me," Sirene cries. The spiny dogfish shark circles Sirene, its teeth bared.

"They're not going to hurt you," Nari says. Her voice is calm. "Not unless I tell them to. But you need to see what you've done."

The sea creatures swim out of the cave. Sirene, Poe and Kate are still contained within their circles. We swim back through the tunnel.

"Wait," Lulu says as we reach the mouth of the tunnel. She swims to the front of the line. I can see her moving the currents. She makes it safe for us to leave the Breakers.

Once we are all free, Lulu lets the currents go back to their normal flow. As we leave, the waters swirl around us, hiding the tunnel from view.

We are a strange band as we make our way back to Ice Canyon. Lulu and Nari swim at the front. They are followed by the first circle of sea creatures, who surround Poe and Kate.

A second, larger circle of creatures contains Sirene, who has not said a word since we left the cave. Dana and I patrol the sides, and Evan swims at the end of the line.

We swim past Fire Canyon on our way home. A number of mer see us and start to follow us.

By the time we reach Ice Canyon, we are a huge group. Most of the Ice Canyon mer come out to see what's going on.

I see Melody's face in the crowd. She has the same look as most of the mer: confusion and concern. I see Bones too. He gives a brief wave. I nod my thanks to him.

"The dome is brighter than I've ever seen it," Nari whispers to me, gazing overhead.

"What color is it?" I ask.

"A lovely blue," Nari says. I follow her gaze, wishing I could see it.

Finally, we reach Ani's cave.

"Lulu?" Ani asks, swooping out to us. "What is all this?"

"We found out who was hurting the sea creatures," Lulu says.

Ani stares at Sirene. "It was you? After the speech you made last night, I should have known."

"Is my father here?" Evan asks.

"I haven't seen him since last night," Ani says. "Someone get Storm."

We wait for twenty minutes, floating in front of the entrance to Ice Canyon. No one says much of anything.

"You!" Storm shouts once he arrives. "And Poe and Kate? I can't believe this."

"Can't you?" Evan asks.

Storm gasps. "What are you saying?"

Evan swims up to his dad. "A few days ago. When we asked about 'X marks the spot,' you looked surprised. But you also looked like you knew something. What was it?"

"You don't think I'm involved, do you?" Storm asks.

Evan shrugs his shoulders. "I don't want to believe it. But I'm not sure."

Storm's face droops. He puts a hand over his eye. He puts another on Evan's shoulder. "I'm sorry," he says. "I saw Sirene near the Breakers a few weeks ago. I knew there were rocks shaped like an X. I suspected Sirene was involved. But I didn't do anything about it."

"Why not?" Even asks.

"I didn't want to think one of the mer would be so foolish as to break the dome and put us all in danger of discovery," he says, loud enough for the tribes to hear.

Then he drops his voice. I am close enough to Evan that I hear what Storm says: "And a part of me wanted to make war on the humans myself, so I didn't investigate."

I shift in the water. Storm looks up and catches my eye.

"And maybe not all humans are bad," he says.

I'm too shocked to say anything. This is the closest Storm has come to saying anything nice to me.

"What happens now?" Lulu asks.

"We punish them," Ani says. "Poe and Kate are Fire Canyon mer. Storm will decide their fates. Sirene belongs to no tribe. Storm and I will decide her fate together."

Ani and Storm withdraw to talk. We all wait. The sea creatures do not break their circle around Sirene. A few of them nudge her. Sirene trembles. Tears roll down her face.

"Are those real tears or fake?" I ask, swimming over to her. I talk to her over the heads of the sea creatures.

Sirene sniffles. She wipes at her tears. "Why did you try to heal me?" she asks.

"I don't know. It seemed like the right thing to do in the moment," I say.

"The right thing," Sirene says. "I thought I was doing the right thing."

"You weren't," I say.

"The mer do not hurt others," Nari says, joining us. "No matter what."

"You used your powers for harm," Dana adds. "There's nothing right about your actions."

Sirene goes silent. No one speaks until Ani and Storm approach.

"We are ready to tell you our decision," Ani says.

"You have been living alone for too long," Storm says. "Some mer are fine on their own, but you are clearly not one of them."

"So what's my punishment?" Sirene asks.

"You will live with the tribes," Storm says. "You will spend part of your time here, at Ice Canyon. And part of your time in Fire Canyon."

"Someone will always be watching you," Ani adds.

I rub my hands together, waiting for the rest of it. They're going to put Sirene in some kind of mer jail at least. I'm surprised when Ani and Storm start swimming away.

"Is that it?" I whisper to Dana.

"Forcing Sirene to live in the community is the worst punishment for her," Dana says. "She wants to be on her own to cause trouble. Now she can't."

"I really don't understand mer ways sometimes," I mumble. Dana squeezes my shoulder and smiles.

Ani and Storm might be done with Sirene, but she's not done with them.

"You speak of community, but you can't live together in one tribe," Sirene says. "You are still separate."

Both Ani and Storm tense and turn back to her.

"That's a fair criticism," Ani says.

"It is," Storm agrees. He looks at Ani. Then he looks at all the mer, who are still here. "And perhaps it is time for a change. Our tribes must work together."

"But not to hurt humans, like Sirene wants," Ani says.

Storm sighs. "I promise that the Fire Canyon will never force the Ice Canyon tribe to hurt humans."

"I suppose that's a start," Ani says. She turns to all of the gathered mer. "I promise that the Ice Canyon tribe will welcome our Fire Canyon brothers and sisters into our lives."

"Not a lot of detail," I comment to Lulu.

"Tell me about it," Lulu says. "But I guess it's something."

"Today marks a new beginning," Ani says. "We might still be two tribes, but today we will start to act as one."

As they begin to leave, most of the mer look confused. A few look concerned. Some of the younger mer, the ones I recognize from the *Clemmons*, look happy.

"We have a lot of details to work out," Storm says as we approach him and Ani.

"I'm proud of you, Mom," Lulu says as she gives Ani a hug.

"You're proud of me? I'm the one who is proud," she says. She hugs all of us, including Evan.

"And here we thought you'd be mad," Dana grins.

"Oh, I *am* mad," Ani says, even as she laughs. "I should be furious that you went to the Breakers on your own. But you also saved the sea creatures. And you helped the tribes. The tribe," she corrects.

"We're not one tribe yet, Ani," Storm says.

"No, but maybe one day," Ani says. To my surprise, Storm nods and squeezes her hand.

"So what about me?" Sirene asks. She sounds whiny.

"You are coming with me," Ani says. "You will live with me for a month. Then you will live at Fire Canyon. We will keep an eye on you." She touches Sirene's arm. "And perhaps one day you will give up this foolish plan of making war on the humans."

Sirene doesn't say anything as Ani leads her away.

Storm nudges Evan. "We need to go home. But you can say goodbye to your friends first."

Storm swims away and turns his back. My friends give Evan quick hugs and tell him they'll see him later at the *Clemmons*.

My heart breaks a little. Will it always be like this? Will I always have to say goodbye to the mer? Will I always be saying goodbye to Evan? I think about when I have to leave Grandpa or when I left my parents this summer. My heart broke then too. Will I always be leaving someone behind?

"Thanks for everything," Evan says as he floats in front of me. "I . . ." His words trail off.

I fling my arms around his neck. "I know," I say.

Evan's arms close around me. I feel like I've come home.

"See you around, India Finch," Evan says as he lets me go.

I smile through my tears. "See you around."

I watch the spot where he disappears long after he's gone. Then I turn to my friends, who wrap me in their arms.

"It's time for me to go home," I say.

CHAPTER 14

The trip home is always faster than the trip to the canyons. When we reach my rock, my friends all give me one last hug.

"I'll miss you so much," Nari says. She is crying more than I am. "But I know you'll be back."

"I will. I promise." I say this every time I leave them. I wonder if one day I'll have to break my promise.

"Next time you can teach me how to swim butterfly," Dana says. This is our joke, since you need two legs to swim the butterfly.

"Definitely," I say. Her red curls swirl in my face as I hug her.

"See you next time," Lulu says. I hug her too.

Then too quickly, they are swimming away, and I am breaking the surface of the water. I pull myself onto a rock. I am hidden from the beach. It always takes a few moments for my lungs to get used to breathing air. My legs and arms feel heavy. They always do after I've been in the water.

When I feel more like a human again, I climb over the rocks toward the beach. I raise my face to the sun. I've missed feeling its warmth.

Grandpa is waiting for me on the beach. He always seems to know when I'm coming home. Sometimes I think he might wait for me every day by the beach.

"India," is all he says. He gives me a quick hug.

"Hi, Grandpa," I say.

"How was it?" he asks.

"Interesting," I say. "I'll tell you about it at dinner. How have things been here?"

"Fine. They've been fine." He carries a walking stick to help him climb over the rocks. "I've had a few visits from Officer Kevin."

"The guy from the beach?" I ask.

"The very same," Grandpa confirms. "I think he's worried you've been jumping off the rocks. I've had to explain why you're never around when he stops by the cabin."

"What did you tell him?" I ask.

"I told him you were at swim camp," he says.

I laugh out loud at this. "Swim camp?"

"Yes, in Portland. I told him you were spending the week at a swim camp in Portland," Grandpa says.

"Okay. You know, I was supposed to be at a swim camp this summer," I say.

Grandpa stops walking. He turns to face me. "I know," he says. "Your parents felt terrible that you had to miss it."

"Have you heard anything from them?" I ask. I don't look at him.

Grandpa puts a hand on my shoulder. "India, they call every single day."

"They do?" I ask, surprised.

Grandpa nods. "They call the visitor center when I'm working a volunteer shift. I don't get reception at the cabin."

"I know," I say. I can't use my phone this entire summer unless I walk to town.

"They miss you terribly. They worry about you," Grandpa says. "Especially your father. He's made me promise to tell him whenever you go to see the mermaids."

"They don't need to worry," I say. "Besides, the tribes are going to try to get along better."

"They are? That's good," Grandpa says. We walk for a few minutes. "India, your parents worry because it's what parents do. It's because they love you."

Our feet crunch over rocks. I wipe away a few tears that escape my eyes.

The sky is blue overhead. The breeze is warm. The ocean crashes as we walk along the beach. Soon we are at Grandpa's cabin. He unlocks the door.

"Welcome home, India."

ABOUT THE AUTHOR

Although **Julie Gilbert's** masterpiece, *The Adventures of Kitty Bob: Alien Warlord Cat*, has sadly been out of print since Julie last stapled it together in the fourth grade, she continues to write. Her short fiction, which has appeared in numerous publications, explores topics ranging from airport security lines to adoption to antique wreaths made of hair. Julie makes her home in southern Minnesota with her husband and two children.

ABOUT THE ILLUSTRATOR

Kirbi Fagan is a vintage-inspired artist living in the Detroit, Michigan, area. She is an award-winning illustrator who specializes in creating art for young readers. She received her bachelor's degree in illustration from Kendall College of Art and Design. Kirbi lives by two words: "Spread joy." She is known to say, "I'm in it with my whole heart." When not illustrating, Kirbi enjoys writing stories, spending time with her family, and rollerblading with her dog, Sophie.

GLOSSARY

carnage (KAR-nij)—a great loss of life, as in a battle

criticism (KRIT-uh-siz-uhm)—a remark that points out fault with something

current (KUR-uhnt)—the movement of water in a definite direction in a river or an ocean

diplomatic (dip-pluh-MA-tik)—tactful and good at dealing with people

habitat (HAB-uh-tat)—the natural place and conditions in which a plant or animals lives

Northern Lights (NOR-thurn lites)—bright, colorful streaks of light that appear in the night sky in the far north

pollution (puh-LOO-shuhn)—harmful materials that damage the air, water, and soil

tide (TIDE)—the constant change in sea level that is caused by the pull of the sun and the moon on the earth

transatlantic cables (trans-at-LAN-tik KAY-buhls)—undersea cables running under the Atlantic Ocean used for communications

vain (VAYN)—having too high an opinion of your appearance, your abilities, or your worth

FURTHER DISCOVERIES

1. In this book, India is an outsider to the mer world even though she is half-mermaid. How does she handle this? Do you think she handles it well?

2. This story is told by India. What if the story was told from Sirene's point of view? How would the story be different?

3. In this book, many of the characters don't see eye to eye. Think of all of the times characters disagreed throughout the story and how they got over their differences. What ways worked better than others?

4. India and her mermaid friends all have different powers. Talk about how their powers relate to their personalities.

5. What real-life people or events are you reminded of by the character or events in the story? Does it make you think of any other books or movies with similar conflicts?

WRITING INSPIRATION

1. All of India's mer friends look different. Write about how you would look if you were a mermaid. What color would your tail be? Would you have a special power?

2. Try writing out India and Lulu's argument from Lulu's point of view. How does Lulu feel about her argument with India? Why does she accuse Evan of being one of the mer who attacked them?

3. In this story, there are two different tribes. Make up your own mer tribe. What is it called? What type of environment do they live in? How do they feel about humans?

4. What if Ani and Storm hadn't calmed down the other mer at the dinner? Write out what you think would have happened if the other mer hadn't listened to them.

JOURNEY EVEN DEEPER INTO...

DARK WATERS

NEPTUNE'S TRIDENT
A MERMAID'S JOURNEY

BY JULIE GILBERT

DARK WATERS

THE SIGHTING
A MERMAID'S JOURNEY

BY JULIE GILBERT

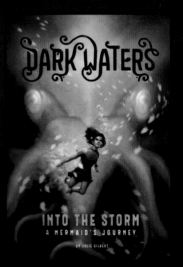

DARK WATERS

INTO THE STORM
A MERMAID'S JOURNEY

BY JULIE GILBERT

DARK WATERS